THE LAST HORIZON

Edited by
Matt Beeson & A J Dalton

kristell-ink.com

All rights reserved. This book or any portion thereof may not be reproduced or used in any manner whatsoever without the express written permission of the publisher except for the use of brief quotations in a book review.

All characters appearing in this work are fictitious. Any resemblance to real persons, living or dead, is purely coincidental.

Pis Aller by J.McDonald © 2022
The Mouse by Nadine Dalton-West© 2022
Snowglobed by Mark Kirkbride © 2022
Charli by John J Ernest © 2022
Burning Ambition by Jodie Hammond © 2022
Mother's Care by Gabriela Houston © 2022
Unicorn Rising by A J Dalton © 2022
Little Fish, Big Pond by Matt Ryder © 2022
Seven Photographs by Huw James © 2022
Ancient Memories, About a Virus by Gabriel Wisdom © 2022
The Cow by Jamie Bear © 2022
At First Bite by Stephen Beeson © 2022
A Day by Amie Angèle Brochu © 2022
The Garden by David Perryman © 2022
Waste by Michael Conroy © 2022
The Fairbourne Witches by Matt Beeson © 2022
The Sacred Grove by Joe Smith © 2022
Seaweed City by Boe Huntress © 2022

ISBN 978-1-913562-38-0 (Hardback)
ISBN 978-1-913562-39-7 (Paperback)
ISBN 978-1-913562-40-3 (EPUB)

Cover art by Charlotte Pang with support from Matt Beeson
Internal images by Gabriela Houston
Typesetting by Book Polishers

Kristell Ink
An Imprint of Grimbold Books

5 St John's Way, Hempton, Oxfordshire, OX15 0QR, United Kingdom
www.kristell-ink.com

For Elissa, Amelie, Leila, Brandon, and all the children grown and growing up in this century, in parallel with our growing understanding of the reality of climate change.

May you be kinder, wiser, and braver than those who came before you.

CONTENTS

Introduction: The Last Horizon by Matt Beeson	3
Pis Aller by J.McDonald	29
The Mouse by Nadine Dalton-West	40
Snowglobed by Mark Kirkbride	51
Charli by John J Ernest	59
Burning Ambition by Jodie Hammond	67
Mother's Care by Gabriela Houston	76
Unicorn Rising by A J Dalton	82
Little Fish, Big Pond by Matt Ryder	91
Seven Photographs by Huw James	108
Ancient Memories, About a Virus by Gabriel Wisdom	121
The Cow by Jamie Bear	128
At First Bite by Stephen Beeson	136
A Day by Amie Angèle Brochu	145
The Garden by David Perryman	154
Waste by Michael Conroy	163
The Fairbourne Witches by Matt Beeson	171
The Sacred Grove by Joe Smith	181
Seaweed City by Boe Huntress	195
About the Authors	207
Acknowledgements	217
A Selection of Other Titles from Kristell Ink	219

INTRODUCTION: THE LAST HORIZON

BY MATT BEESON

'Humanity is at a crossroads' could be the start of any number of science fiction stories. Unfortunately for humanity, as a cursory google of the phrase will reveal, we appear to be living through our very own science fiction story. The decisions that individuals, communities, and nations make now will have a profound effect on our future. Recently on BBC Radio 4's 'The Climate Tipping Points[1]', climate futurist and author Alex Steffen said:

'In another hundred years it's going to be obvious that the moment we're in right now is an inflection point. There is a huge gap between what most of us understand about the

---

1 BBC Radio 4's 'The Climate Tipping Points' is available at: https://www.bbc.co.uk/sounds/play/m00181m0

planetary crisis we face and the magnitude of that crisis. There's no future that we have ahead of us now where climate change, ecological decline, [and] toxic pollution aren't massive problems, because they already are. And I think hundreds of millions of people are in the process of going through that recognition of reality and I think once that happens there's the very real possibility of transformations in our economy [and] in our politics that seem deeply improbable now…'

Science fiction stories have always provided a means to consider the future, scraping diligently at the vast surface of an infinite variety of possibilities. *The Last Horizon* compilation is partly inspired by the notion that such stories are stained-glass windows on the multiverse, helping us to imagine, if nothing else, the importance of our decisions in the present, while at the same time helping us to escape from the burdens of it.

The thing that these stories often (if not always!) have in common is that they have humans in them. The spectrum of suffering for these putative future folk is somewhat broad. At one end of this range, spawned from the profound Western optimism of the late 1980s/early 1990s comes the approaching-utopian: *Star Trek: The Next Generation*. The other end – let's call it the violet end, because it has a higher energy – is described well by a range of titles, all exploring their own particular vision. Each, perhaps, is the product of decisions (or even a singular decision) made at some point in a world-constructed history that varies in nebulosity but contextualises the story and guides the characters through inspiration and tradition.

Fiction inspired by climate change remains relatively thin on the ground, the most obvious example being 2019's *The Wall* by John Lanchester. This is followed in 2021 by Rosa Rankin-Gee's *Dreamland*. *The Wall* is set in a world where the ravages of climate change are evident; the sea levels have risen, and the titular wall is a polder dike holding back both the water and refugees. *Dreamland* could be the spiritual prequel, set as the sea levels are rising and the political climate is gravitating towards a right wing that embraces dysgenic ideology, all while the people of Thanet try to get on with *normal* life. In 2014, Zadie Smith published a short piece in the *New York Review*[2], 'An Elegy for a Country's Seasons'. She writes:

> *People in mourning tend to use euphemism; likewise the guilty and ashamed. The most melancholy of all the euphemisms: "The new normal." "It's the new normal," I think, as a beloved pear tree, half-drowned, loses its grip on the earth and falls over. The train line to Cornwall washes away—the new normal. We can't even say the word "abnormal" to each other out loud: it reminds us of what came before. Better to forget what once was normal, the way season followed season, with a temperate charm only the poets appreciated.*

Notwithstanding the relatively smaller quantity of clear climate change inspired fiction, there has never been a shortage of dystopian fiction that considers the effect on freedom and democracy brought about by some increased scarcity of valuable resources. *The Handmaid's Tale* by Margaret Atwood, recently an exceptional television dramatisation, is a perfect illustration of the potential for prescience in literature (the novel written originally in the 1980s). While Atwood is credited with saying that since publication all of the horrors she envisaged have come to pass in some way, somewhere, there are many who fear that Gilead is on the cusp of terrible

---

2 Zadie Smith's short is available online from *The New York Review:* https://www.nybooks.com/articles/2014/04/03/elegy-countrys-seasons

transition from fiction to reality, not by revolution as Atwood's original text supposes, but by laws implemented by democratic institutions. Sammy HK Smith's *Anna* describes the descent of a nation state into a fractured society, in an abusive relationship with itself; once national structure, institutions, and policing are taken away, only the politics of physical power remain. *The Wall* is similar in the way it pulls on threads of the present to imagine a dark future. The current (at time of writing in 2022) UK government's hostile attitude towards asylum seekers and economic migrants becomes a wall upon which *Defenders* wait for *Others* to attempt to cross. John Lanchester says in interview[3] that his novel is:

> *'a version of the possible future in which a lot of current trends are scrolled forwards. The main ones being about [...] unchecked climate change carrying on in the way that we already know it is and the other one being that tendency to walls and fortifications and divisions between nations and the premise is a world in which climate change has so impacted the UK [...] and the UK is kind of a fortress state.'*

The author who sets their stories in a future time will often pull on threads of the present, and weave them into the tapestry of the possible, positioned somewhere on that spectrum of suffering from *Star Trek NG* to 'It's only cats left now and frankly we're better off without you ridiculous bipeds'[4]. Fiction inspired by climate change, indeed such as this compilation, carries with it an

---

[3] The interview with John Lanchester can be viewed here: https://www.youtube.com/watch?v=4PBoT3LkWh8

[4] Netflix series *Love Death Robots*, the first episodes of Seasons 1 and 3 (Three Robots and Three Robots: Exit Strategies, respectively) encapsulates the sci-fi vision and warning. Money and power will only get you so far – perhaps to Mars, until the cats take over!

inherent darkness. This darkness comes from the knowledge that climate change is actually happening, right now. This means that climate fiction (or 'cli-fi' as it's popularly termed) may not always provide the same degree of escapism as other futuristic fiction. If it pays sufficient homage to the science as per best current understanding, it carries with it the constant nagging reminder that – if there isn't a huge shift in attitudes and policies – the vision of the future may be only all too realistic.

In the case of *Dreamland*, this is agonisingly visceral and plausible. Rankin-Gee plucks on the threads of right-wing policies currently observable in Western democracies and loops them into a near future vision of fascism that is ofttimes gentle but nonetheless insistent and brutal, that justifies itself on the basis that it is saving the-people-that-need-saving. Unless checked and mitigated climate change will bring about the massive displacement and migration that *The Wall* describes. For now, our future remains within our control. But if you close your eyes and listen closely, you will surely hear the sound of the sands of our agency rushing through the cracks in our resolve to the abyss beneath.

There are those who believe that nations should attempt to adapt to climate change, rather than trying to prevent it, that the cost of prevention is too high both financially and socially. The truth of this, however, is that no *nation* can adapt to the huge level of migration predicted (not at least without the level of political reorganisation that Atwood, Lanchester, Rankin-Gee, and many others suggest). The prediction of the number of people that could be displaced by 2050 varies; 200 million people is an often-quoted figure. One prediction from the Institute for Economics and Peace (IEP), described in *The Guardian*[5], predicts as many as 1.2 billion. Either way, it's a big

---

5 Again, if interested, the Guardian article that considers displacement of people can be read here: https://www.theguardian.com/environment/2020/sep/09/climate-crisis-could-displace-12bn-people-by-2050-report-warns

number. And a huge amount of avoidable suffering.

The story may well be different for the wealthy and connected. The *walls* that are built might not be the grand constructions around entire nations of Lanchester's vision, but smaller, more modest affairs encompassing only, say, a billionaire's estate. We should be circumspect of anyone who tells us that the cost of prevention of climate change is too great, no matter how enticing the idea of carrying on as normal may be. If the cost is not borne now by the people and organisations with the resources to bear it, then it will ultimately be borne by the rest of us, or our children and grandchildren. Adapting a mansion estate might involve building a wall; adapting family homes to floods, drinking water scarcity, food shortages, and mass migration and war over increasingly scarce resources involves significantly greater sacrifice.

All of this suffering *is* avoidable. Climate change is in part a technical problem, but most of all it is a human problem. Introducing Axiom No. 1:

Climate change is not a ___ problem, it's a human one!

Actually, even when it is a technical problem it's still a human problem! Take the problem of synthesis of diverse and multi-disciplinary fields, for example. Most of all, it is a problem of communication and organisation; it's a problem of empathy. The technical perspective is the one that gets the most airtime and, indeed, significant grounds for optimism can be found in the rise of 'clean' or 'green' technologies: wind turbines, electric cars, batteries, solar panels, the generation of hydrogen by electrolysis, carbon capture and storage, even humble home insulation, the list goes on. All of the technology we need to address climate change and avoid huge suffering is already available to us, with a slightly varying degree of technological readiness[6] for some variants of particular technologies. There is really no need to go chasing metaphorical unicorns[7].

All technologies have their proponents and their detractors. One of the common criticisms levelled at this development is the use of the words 'clean' and / or 'green'; the all too familiar on Twitter: 'look at that burning wind turbine, that's so green. It used so much energy and carbon to get it there in the first place and now it's on fire, it'll never pay back the invested energy. Give me a good coal plant any day' and so on and tiresomely on. Despite the obvious and necessary responses around the massively advantageous period of return on carbon investment and low frequency at which such fires occur, there is some objective sympathy to be had with this reaction. These technologies are not (yet) truly green or clean and terming them such helps fuel the rise of a new beast: The Energy Transition Detractor (more on him – and they do so often tend to be *him* – in a moment). These technologies are arguably sticking plasters, or a better analogy: the tourniquet that humanity needs to get us through the next hundred years without making the planet entirely unliveable. The lithium mines are a blight on our planet, both environmentally and often socially, the rare earths similarly so, geologically stored carbon might need to be stored in areas where it has some potential to leak out again, solar panels use up land that could

---

6 Technological readiness level is generally scored from 1-9, where 1 is a raw idea, 7 is proof of concept, and 9 is fully market ready. Many of the technologies listed are 9s, although you could argue that large scale carbon capture or floating wind are a 7 or 8, and generation of hydrogen by electrolysing seawater is more likely to be 5 or 6.

7 Unicorns are a popular tech metaphor for privately held start-up businesses valued at $1 billion USD or more. While there could potentially be a 'unicorn' that is beneficial for mitigating climate change because of something new and innovative, we don't *need* one.

be otherwise used for farming[8], and wind turbines really do kill birds. These downsides, and there are more – the list could indeed go on; all technologies are imperfect and come with a cost – pale in comparison to the threat that we face as a species from climate change.

This tourniquet analogy helps to put solutions into perspective, particularly variants of nuclear fission. Lily Cole writes in *Who Cares Wins* that 'Nu-clear remains un-clear' for her, largely because of the finite supply of uranium: 135 years as Cole postulates. There is obvious and sensible sympathy to be had with these concerns. Why should we solve one problem, only to generate more problems for our future selves (nuclear waste, mining scars, environmental pollution)? The answer is that these are lower order problems; they are a lower priority. Failing to solve the problem of dangerous climate change means that we will not have the *privilege* of being able to worry about these other concerns. Focussing too greatly on one technological or political approach risks putting all of the eggs of our tourniquet's ecological harm in one basket. In truth all of this must be balanced, potentially, for example, through the generation of nuclear waste to offset lithium mining; spread the love.

Axiom number 1 is arguably the best defence and justification for a balanced technological and strategic approach. Historical examples from mining industries show that it can take longer than a generation to retrain and repurpose an industry. There is a huge amount of mistrust of large oil and gas industries, and this is understandable. However, the expertise these organisations offer can be very useful for the clean technology transition. Why not allow people to gravitate towards their area

---

8 Having said that solar panels use up land that could be otherwise used for farming, there's quite some discussion (if not a huge volume of evidence) to suggest that soil health improves as a result of not being intensively farmed while solar farms are installed, alongside the benefits for pollinators, birds, and other wildlife.

of competence and interest? Why not leverage the techniques and expertise available in these 'dirty' industries to support the clean energy transition? Offshore experience, for example, in the North Sea oilfields, translates well to Offshore Wind (where we can build very tall turbines without encountering nimbyist wrath) with regards to logistics and access. Oil and gas companies have geotechnical expertise that is very useful for understanding the capability to store carbon in the subsurface, potentially in depleted oil and gas reservoirs. Hydrogen gas has been used safely and effectively in refineries for decades. This shouldn't be seen as a defence of large multinational oil and gas companies and the huge profits they make; they are, after all, the historical enablers of climate change, a big reason why we are here now. But we *are* here, and we can't go back and change that (or can we?). It doesn't make sense to tear things down for the sake of it, when competence and experience, both individual and organisational, can be put to better use.

Balance in technological approach also creates balance in a human sense. Oil and gas companies, nuclear companies, coal mining, and higher carbon industries all provide jobs that we can't just scrap if we're to provide a kind, socially sound energy transition (more on this later). We can't afford a generation to retrain people either. People who take a purist environmental view of the climate change problem perhaps don't have a full appreciation of the real urgency of action required. We can't afford to be picky over which low carbon technologies we use. We can't have green infighting over which solution is best (returning to Axiom No. 1!). Lily Cole and others may well be, understandably, unclear about nuclear, but she is crystal where is matters:

> *"There is no more urgent need in the world today than to stop burning fossil fuels."*

Humans are a species that is uniquely social and verbal. Stories, our love for them and our ability to tell them, define who we are. There's very little about civilisation that doesn't revolve around some kind of story that we tell ourselves. To introduce Axiom No. 2:

There is nothing more human than the telling of stories.

There doesn't seem a huge amount of value in attempting to prove this axiom in these pages. If you want to think about this further, then a very good thought-provoking read can be found in *Sapiens* by Yuval Noah Harari[9]. If you don't see the value of stories, then *The Last Horizon* probably isn't for you, it being a collection of stories inspired by climate change. Despite any indication to the contrary that you may have received from the preceding paragraphs, dear Reader, please be assured that this book is not a polemic. It is not intended to change your mind or reinforce your perspective. It is intended to tell stories of a particularly human catastrophe / problem / opportunity, or however we may wish to frame the anthropogenic changes to our climate and the awareness we have of these changes brought about through human science. Climate change is ostensibly remote, both spatially and temporally; telling the stories of climate change may make it less so. It is also intended to tell you stories that are enjoyable and interesting. However, if by any chance it should also spark an idea, provide a glimmer of inspiration, or nurture a shoot of empathy and kindness then so much the better. Introducing Axiom No. 3:

Telling the stories of climate change is important.

---

[9] *Sapiens* is a good read and it's very thought provoking. Don't go incurring Dr Adam Rutherford's wrath by taking the 'science' in it too seriously on Twitter though.

Why is it important to tell the stories of climate change? In a nutshell, because presenting the science isn't enough. It's demonstrably insufficient, not because there's anything wrong with the science, because there isn't. It's more because we live in a society that frequently prefers to ignore the science or labels it Leftist when it contradicts our preconceived notions of truth. Particularly when there are influential people who are unabashed in telling their own story, of how the cost of combatting climate change, the cost of net zero is too great. Nigel Farage tweeted on 2 March 2022, in response to a *Telegraph* article with the headline 'Government has 'no idea' how much its net zero plans will cost Britain':

Time to end the net zero madness of Mrs [sic] Johnson.

And on 6 March:

We need a referendum on the net zero madness… The Richmond Greens don't have to worry about paying their gas bills – but millions of ordinary people do.

Farage claims that the cost of net zero is too great for the nation to bear. There are innumerable rational arguments – some of which are presented in this introduction – that refute this notion. Not least of them is that Farage and those of his ilk are agents of chaos who have ably demonstrated in recent years that their only real beliefs and causes hold low orbit around their own self-aggrandisement. But if there *was* a referendum tomorrow, how would you vote? How would your family vote? Does the purely scientific perspective give you enough of an understanding of the implications of climate change?

Science fiction also provides an insight into the effects of listening to people like Farage. *The Wall*, *The Handmaid's Tale*,

Dreamland, Bradbury's *Fahrenheit 451*, Orwell's *1984*, Suzanne Collins's *The Hunger Games*, and many more all show the increased authoritarianism that comes from having to *adapt* to environmental changes rather than preventing them. Readers are left with an image of elites who will be able to survive and adapt. It's not difficult to imagine that individuals with resources really can adapt; it's much easier to build a wall around an estate than it is to build one around an entire nation, employing the lucky few who get to work the land and defend the walls. There's no question that this is a short-sighted view, but it has the advantage of generating a comforting illusion of self-reliance – one with which, no doubt, the modern billionaire is familiar – of not needing to engage with politics and differing views. That said, Farage is no billionaire; he's a real-life Loki without the magic or charisma, but the sad and dangerous thing is that he doesn't need magic or charisma when his message presents easy ignorance as an alternative to difficult change.

Farage employs another familiar dog whistle in his tweets: 'The Richmond Greens…' Obviously he's trying to generate division here; he wants us to see green activism as another form of privilege, the domain of wealthy elites, not *ordinary* folk as he ostensibly sees himself. His timing is rarely accidental. At the time of writing (June 2022), there is a noticeable backlash against climate change protestors. The protests are often inconvenient (well, deliberately so!) and obstructive. Farage and his malignant brethren, supported by legislation introduced by the propaganda machine masquerading as a UK government, seek to generate a hostile climate for people who want to exercise their democratic right to protest, including the people who really believe in the urgency of our predicament, to drive a wedge between 'the loony green brigade' and ordinary-hard-working-people-who-just-want-to-get-on-with-our-lives.

While most people fall into the second camp – because, hey, who has the time? – most people also want to have children and grandchildren with a reasonable chance of a future. These protestors that we vilify and curse when they make us late for work are our conscience-credit trading scheme. They do the work that we can't (or won't).

The sad irony here is that (remember Axiom No. 1) climate change isn't quite the same as other environmental issues. No one is trying to 'save the planet'. The planet doesn't care; it's been through this before[10]. Earth will survive and crack on with or without us. And there's the nub; as things currently stand, it'll be without us (save perhaps a few lucky folk in their walled, environment-controlled mansions and the servants who wipe their posteriors and man the gates). *Civilisation* won't survive.

Often protesters are accused of hypocrisy, particularly when travelling around the world to protest and increasing their own personal carbon footprint in the process. In *Who Cares Wins* Lily Cole explains that it is difficult (if not impossible) to avoid hypocrisy in the modern world. We all need to get to work, and eat, and live comfortably, and have holidays. This is true on an individual level and emphasises the importance of community and government action. There is another way to escape hypocrisy: deny that climate change is happening, or deny that it's anthropogenic, or more commonly of late accept the former but deny that there's anything we can do about it. This leads to a conclusion that there is a Venn diagram that describes two camps of modern humans: hypocrites and arseholes. This book is aimed primarily at the former. None of this is to say that there isn't a spectrum of hypocrisy. *Who Cares Wins* is an excellent and sensible exploration of things we can do as individuals to reduce our impact in a number of areas, including our carbon footprint.

---

10 In the Eocene CO_2 levels were ~4-5 x higher than today.

Zadie Smith is one of the UK's most respected authors. BBC Radio 4 recently ran a programme[11] where she reads excerpts from her novels, accompanied and supported by the BBC Symphony Philharmonic Orchestra playing selected pieces of music. She used that platform to describe her attitude to climate protestors:

> *'It's Earth Day today, and Earth Day makes me want to say something very quickly while I'm up here, with what the kids call a platform. A lot of people my age, including me, often find themselves giving the side-eye to young people or complaining about them in one way or another. But for number 1, they've obviously grown up facing the total extinction of the planet and, number 2, not a few of them have been busy chaining themselves to buildings, blocking bridges, shutting down traffic, and protesting in airports, and generally civically revolting in the exact same time period that I have been, let's face it, writing novels. Recently, I read that the UN Secretary General called the latest IPCC report 'a file of shame, cataloguing the empty pledges that put us firmly on track towards an unliveable world.' If we have any chance of avoiding that unliveable world, or more realistically at this point somewhat lessening its unliveability, it will be because of the climate activists, many of them young, who are presently doing the only thing that really matters. I am in their debt. We all are.'*

'The only thing that really matters.' People who are willing to take civic action to highlight the dangers that we all face from inaction, or delayed action, are one of our most critically scarce resources. If they need to fly from place to place in order to protest, then that's almost certainly good value from

---

11 BBC Radio 4's Zadie Smith and the BBC Symphony Orchestra is Available at: https://www.bbc.co.uk/sounds/play/m0016wzp

the perspective of avoiding dangerous climate change. The trade-off is net negative, let alone net zero. Eventually, of course, the goal is to achieve home-grown-climate-protestor self-sufficiency, reduce the protestor-miles necessary for a well organised, efficacious protest, but until then...

In the BBC's 'The Climate Tipping Points', Alex Steffen, after reflecting that, in a hundred years, it will be obvious that societies now are developing the systems and structures to deal with climate change, goes on to talk about the reasons why it is so difficult to take action on climate change, 'even though it's blindingly obvious that it's happening and that it's only going to get worse':

'The big thing to understand about the politics of climate change is that they're the politics of tempo. Everybody who is informed understands that we're going to be making big changes, but how quickly we make those changes matters. And for people who are heavily invested in, say, fossil fuels or unsustainable agriculture or waterfront real estate, the slower we make these changes, the more money they make in the meantime. And so, for some people, delaying the pace of change is all important. But the delay that they are engaging in affects everyone else. It's harmful to most humans and everybody coming in the future, so it's not a neutral delay, it's a predatory delay. And we're facing that predatory delay all around, whether we're talking climate science denialists, or conservatives in the US who want to block the expansion of clean energy, or people who are ignoring the risk of big storms and rising seas to waterfront real estate.'

The people that Steffen refers to in the above quote – he terms them the 'Climate Lobby' – are mostly good examples of the *arseholes* in our scheme above. Our anger at climate change protesters, when taken in full context, does seem a trifle misplaced. In truth, in a hundred years' time, they are the people who will be printed on banknotes, if we still have banknotes, the Millicent Fawcetts to whom we will erect statues, and make speeches in front of[12], about whatever our next existential threat might be.

Cli-fi is different to traditional sci-fi. With a few of the differences that we've touched on already, for example within the escapism of reading a good story, we can perhaps feel this nugget of anxiety: 'Shit, this could actually be real.' In that way perhaps, while cli-fi tends to gravitate to the near future it is, arguably, more science-based than it is about differences in science or technology. The cli-fi examples described in the preceding pages speculate heavily on the nature of society, and how climate change might affect the way people interact. Remembering our Axioms 1 and 2, *The Last Horizon* compilation muses on a number of dystopian visions and also a number of human aspects, for example, the nature of empathy, sympathy and compassion; is empathy something that is purely reserved for human people who are proximal to ourselves, or can it be extended to consider humans who live in other parts of the world or other animals? This sort of question runs to the very heart of what it means to be human, and what it means to tell stories. Certain political movements of recent years would suggest a desire to close in rather than reach out. But isn't this to be expected? Doesn't this expose the link to economic success, societal meritocracy and the capacity and desire to

---

12 'Speeches in front of Millicent Fawcett' is a reference to the 'Declaration of Rebellion' in 2018, when George Monbiot, Caroline Lucas, and in particular, Greta Thunberg made speeches in front of the statue in London's Parliament Square (there are also statues of Gandhi and Nelson Mandela). Everyone mentioned in this footnote deserves significantly more than a footnote.

reach out further with compassion? Rosa Rankin-Gee explores this link in *Dreamland*, when she writes:

> *'What do you even mean "my dad is"?' But you didn't need to answer. Those three words already said everything. Where you start, where you end up.'*

As we've covered, futuristic fiction often builds on tendencies that already exist in society. While *Dreamland* is set in a future Thanet, it speaks to social divisions in the UK and around the world. Many authors, such is Hashi Mohamed in *People Like Us*, write about the myth of meritocracy, how the single greatest determining factor of future success is where you started from. The self-perpetuating glass floor only allows through the exceptions to this rule. These exceptions – such as self-professed exception Hashi Mohamed, now a successful barrister who came from Somalia as a refugee aged nine, not speaking a word of English – are held up by elites as great examples of our thriving meritocracy, effectively gaslighting, selling the dream, the possibility of success regardless of your background. Everyone loves a story of success (almost as much as we love a story of hubris and failure due to reaching above our station?).

Climate change is a human problem (Axiom No. 1). The human tendency to *other* will not be mercifully ignored by changes to society that result from climate change. In fact, we've already seen it several times in the history of humanity, not least during the Dust Bowl and the Great Depression. Steinbeck's *Grapes of Wrath* (arguably the first example of cli-fi) presents it to you in beautiful, heart-wrenching detail. The people migrating from Oklahoma because of the changes to living conditions caused by the dust bowl are just Okies to the folk in California; they're not the people-who-are-worth-saving, as Rankin-Gee might describe them in *Dreamland*.

Humans are very gifted in finding reasons to *other*. We prioritise care for people who are like ourselves, mental gymnastics that people will exercise to dehumanise other groups of people (and other sentient beings, not just people) – often disadvantaged in some way – to justify callousness or downright cruelty. No matter what they may or may not espouse to the contrary, all of the world's governments know what is coming as a result of climate change, the UK government included. The inhumane and shameful attitude (at time of writing there is consideration to send individuals to Rwanda for 'processing') to what is a relative trickle of refugees could well be intended to avoid setting a human kindness precedent that will need to be stretched beyond recognition in the decades to come. The floods from the rains and the sea level rise are nothing to the flood of human suffering that will break on all our shores. Climate change is not a crisis for the planet: it is a crisis for humankind, for all people, and we must rise to meet it as humans and people.

It's not all doom and gloom, and it definitely doesn't have to be. It never had to be. We just need to listen to the people screaming about the urgency of our predicament, to be tolerant of the people who are making the points that need to be made on behalf of all of us. As we've covered, we have the technology we need to make a difference: we just need to roll it out more quickly (net zero by 2050 is too late and, frankly, we need to be talking net negative, taking greenhouse gases out of the atmosphere). *New Scientist* recently wrote about the UK producing more electricity than it needs by 2030[13], perhaps hinting at great opportunity to lead, exporting excess energy to continental Europe and/or generating hydrogen from

---

[13] New Scientist article about producing more energy than needed by 2030: Quite a good article actually: https://www.newscientist.com/article/2320812

electrolysis using the surplus. And there are other enabling technologies that can definitely help. The stuff of traditional sci-fi (AI, Quantum Computing, Nuclear Fusion) will play a part, if we can do enough of the more mundane to give them the room to come to fruition. These technologies are achieving astounding developments every day, but carbon emissions need to start coming down yesterday; as things stand, they're still going up today and they will be tomorrow. The Intergovernmental Panel on Climate Change (IPCC) report[14] highlights that unless deep cuts are made in emissions right now then we're likely to hit the 1.5°C warming target of the 2015 Paris Agreement by 2034, sixteen years before many nations are committing to reduce emissions to net zero. Alex Steffen's *predatory delay* risks eating its own self-interest, and he goes on to say:

> *'What is happening is that there are millions and millions of people, and very powerful institutions, who are realising that their direct self-interest relies on acting more quickly than we're used to thinking about. And that is everything from investment banks that are funding clean energy looking to avoid having their assets dissipate in a carbon crash all the way down to a local government understanding that we need to think now about flooding and fire and storms and protect citizens accordingly. Most of the reasons we need to act aren't altruistic but offer people the chance to be better protected against pretty dire problems, to get a better return on their investment, to find a new job, to create a new industry. And the competition to create the new is at least as strong a force, right now, as the opposition to change in the first place. And we can see that all across the landscape. We can see that in clean energy, in electrification,*

---

14 The IPCC report is described in this BBC article: https://www.bbc.com/news/science-environment-58130705

we can see it in vehicle design, we can see it in transportation systems and agricultural systems. Everywhere you look there are innovations surging forward and as they surge forward they're getting better and cheaper.'

The politics of tempo. Encourage, don't vilify protestors who ask us to move more quickly. Support social change, a Green New Deal (named for Franklin D. Roosevelt's New Deal that came out of the Great Depression) to help ensure that the energy transition is a kind transition, that we create jobs rather than destroying them. This could be such a time of great optimism, a global blitz spirit as we rise as all humanity to deliver the technology, societal, systems change that we need to deliver in order to win the war on climate change. Maybe the only reason why climate change is such a bleak and depressing subject is because the status quo, including big oil and governments that depend on big oil, tells us it is? It doesn't need to be. *This* could be the real story of climate change.

The mitigation of climate change through the use of different, low carbon technology for power generation (wind, solar, tidal, nuclear) and the use of technology to remove CO_2 directly from the air or from produced gas, and then using it or storing it, are large important components of the drive to net zero. These approaches can help to remove or compensate for the embedded carbon in the products we buy and the lives that we live. However, there is still work to be done to make these approaches fully sustainable. *Sustainability* is a word that often accompanies discussions around the net zero energy transition, but it actually embodies a much wider subject. Sustainability is best defined by the seventeen UN Sustainability Goals[15], of which Clean and Affordable Energy, and Climate Action are

---

15 The UN Sustainability Goals can be found here: https://sdgs.un.org/goals

goals 7 & 13, respectively (note the *and affordable* part of goal 7).

Sustainability for clean energy will include other aspects too, such as low carbon steel for wind turbines, where steel is produced from hydrogen rather than coal, or such as fully recyclable batteries (also forming part of goal 12 – Ensure Sustainable Production and Consumption Patterns). Quickly building a sustainable world will not only help to mitigate dangerous climate change but will also ensure that today's tourniquet doesn't become tomorrow's noose.

Interestingly, another phrase that is used frequently in conjunction with sustainability and the net zero transition is *carbon offsetting*. This is the process by which we can pay an amount of money to offset our carbon emissions, for example, from a flight. The money we pay becomes part of a fund that might support a clean energy or afforestation project. This process is not superficially dissimilar to the process of buying indulgences for our sins in the Middle Ages, an interesting way of interpreting the 'eye of the needle' parable! But, anyway, then as now, the wealthy could commit sins and cough up the cash to make God or the climate turn a blind eye.

Cynicism aside, carbon offsetting is not 100% a con, but nor is it as easy and obvious a fix as it is sometimes purported. If we spend time thinking about the projects we want to invest in to offset our carbon emissions, for example, in the UK, making sure that afforestation projects comply with the guidelines of the Woodland Trust, then it can be very beneficial. However, it is arguably at odds with building a sustainable world. The emissions are still being generated: it's just now there is a Carbon Offsetting investment fund that can be used to help mitigate *future* emissions. This is definitely all part of the 'we need everything, and we need it now' rationale, but it can't replace good old fashioned social responsibility.

It's also worth being selective over offsetting schemes. As

with any industry, there are providers who are scrupulously following scientific principles and there might be those who are less scrupulous or misguided. Planting trees is the stereotypical carbon offsetting idea (there are others, such as peat restoration or funding renewable energy projects); what could be a better way of removing carbon from the air and storing it than nature's very own lungs: forests? Trees are great, take a quote, but only when we consider the soil first. Most carbon is in fact sequestered below ground, in significantly less huggable soil[16]. There is a danger that intensive afforestation could release more carbon due to disturbing high-quality soil than is sequestered over time as trees grow: that's why it's important to baseline the soil first and only engage in planting in poorer soil. Supporting schemes that take this into account could well help to mitigate future carbon emissions. Governments around the world provide guidance, as with, for example, the Environment Agency's 'Achieving net zero – A review of the evidence behind potential carbon offsetting approaches' [17], which refers to the Woodland Carbon Code. The story of soil is one that we don't often hear told (because, let's face it, it's soil!) but it's an incredibly important part of the mix: it's, quite literally, the earth itself.

Hopefully, some of the above discussions serve to illustrate the social divide that we face in relation to climate change, not just in terms of who will bear the potential consequences, but the unequal distribution of individual agency in the mitigation

---

16 It's not just soil. Check out this infographic: https://www.visualcapitalist.com/sp/visualizing-carbon-storage-in-earths-ecosystems/ 'Soil contains almost 2X as much of carbon as the atmosphere and living flora and animals combined.'

17 If you're really interested, the EA's 'Achieving net zero – A review of the evidence behind potential carbon offsetting approaches' is here: https://assets.publishing.service.gov.uk/media/60cc698cd3bf7f4bcb0efe02/Achieving_net_zero_-_a_review_of_the_evidence_behind_carbon_offsetting_-_report.pdf

of climate change. This inequality is what nefarious characters like Nigel Farage are attempting to exploit. People who have moderate financial resources can afford to: buy sustainably, go vegan, avoid palm oil, pay for carbon offsetting, buy solar panels, buy electric cars, and switch to heat pumps. Without wanting to prejudge AT ALL, if you're frequenting a foodbank in Tory UK, it's *probably* less likely that you're going to worry about trying to stay vegan. You've got more immediate – if not bigger – things to worry about. This is why individual action, while wonderful, can only go so far without government policy support, which frankly – not just in the UK but around the world – seldom amounts to more than the lip service necessary to satisfy the majority of disinterested folk of your governmental green credentials, no offence intended.

There's no question that agency and ready cash are positively correlated. That's not to say that, just because we can't afford something – either in money or time – right now, doesn't mean we shouldn't aspire to it. *Personal Pronoun Alert* I, for example, am an *aspiring* vegan. I acknowledge that being vegan is a morally superior position to take (this is pretty objectively true, really, from a health, animal welfare, and climate change perspective) but I also acknowledge my own hypocrisy: I can't seem to find the time to organise myself sufficiently to plan to eat without eggs and cheese occasionally. I'm in the hypocrite camp, not the arsehole camp. I think. Most of the time anyway. I think it's ok to know the right thing to do, but to give yourself a break if you can't always get there. Don't give the government a break though, not for a second.

There are a lot of stories that need to be told (not just soil's!). Human stories about displacement, migration, and seeking refuge. Human stories of the kindness of those who will help, no matter what the cost. Technological stories of how we prevent, survive, and adapt. Elegiac mourning stories for what we have already lost and what we have yet to lose. Stories of the consequences, of fire, drought, viruses, and famine. Stories of cooperation, stories of empathy, stories of what the absence of those things can lead to.

Remember the three axioms:

1) Climate change is not a ___ problem, it's a human one!
2) There is nothing more human than the telling of stories.
3) Telling the stories of climate change is important.

And perhaps a fourth one:

4) It's ok to know the right thing and not be able to do it *right* now. You can still aspire to it!

This compilation of stories could have been called a number of different things. Perhaps, in keeping with the tradition of Dr Dalton's excellent and successful 'Book of' series ('The Book of Changes', or perhaps more fitting 'The Book of Consequences)', *The Last Horizon* was proposed as a working title that – as is often the way of these things – stuck stubborn and immovable, growing in connotation as the stories were submitted and compiled. We are approaching the last horizon, getting closer every day, the point beyond which there may be no return. Humanity is at a crossroads, the premise of many works of fiction. Only this time, it's for real.

Postscript – 30th June, 2022

It is very difficult to keep up with the pace of change in the world at the moment. And not all of it is going in the *right* direction. In the two weeks or so since I finished my final draft of this piece, quite a lot has happened. There are two things, in particular, that are relevant to points made in the preceding pages. Firstly, the Supreme Court in America has effectively overturned the 1973 Roe vs Wade judgement, that effectively granted the right to abortion to women across the United States of America. The removal of this right has led many to comment that women's bodies are now more regulated than guns. Secondly, 'Brexit Man' Steve Bray was arrested while undertaking a peaceful protest outside of the UK Parliament in Westminster. The Guardian[18] writes:

> *The Police, Crime, Sentencing and Courts Act, which came into force on Tuesday, introduces an offence of intentionally or recklessly causing public nuisance, in an attempt to crack down on disruptive guerrilla protests of the kind used by climate change activists.*

Steve Bray has been peacefully protesting Brexit outside of parliament since 2018. While the Metropolitan police claim he was arrested for violating a 2011 statute, the timing with respect to the new act seems suspicious. What does this new act mean in practice for climate change protestors? Time will tell but taking a long view of the need for change, it seems to me that we need more protests right now, not less. We certainly don't need to be arresting and deterring the people who see humanity's predicament most clearly.

It feels very much like everyone who has even a hint of power should read science fiction novels. *The Handmaid's Tale*, and its sequel *The Testaments*, in particular, should be a qualifying pre-requisite for anyone running for public office, anywhere in the world. That said, I'm fairly certain that Margaret Atwood intended her novels to be a warning, rather than a how-to guide.

---

18 Guardian article about Steve Bray arrest: https://www.theguardian.com/uk-news/2022/jun/28/police-swoop-on-stop-brexit-man-under-new-anti-protest-law

The great Martin Luther King told us that '…the arc of the moral universe is long but it bends toward justice.' This may or may not be true, but what this doesn't mean is that people who want change for what they see as the better can wait for it to happen. Justice means different things to different people[19], and *climate justice* is too often conflated with inconvenience and annoyance, perhaps too much so for it even to be included in many people's understanding of that quote. If you are encumbered by your own developing or established sense of the meaning of the word *justice* (whether or not this book has helped or hindered this in any way), it's important to remember that many people in the world are already working to bend the arc of history toward their own definition. Don't get left behind.

Post-Postscript – 30th June, 2022 (a bit later on)

Fuckers. Supreme Court fuckers[20]:

In a 6-3 decision that will seriously hinder America's ability to stave off disastrous global heating, the supreme court, which became dominated by rightwing justices under the Trump administration, has opted to support a case brought by West Virginia that demands the US Environmental Protection Agency (EPA) be limited in how it regulates planet-heating gases from the energy sector.

Fuckers.
Not the end.

---

19 A good Huffington Post article that warns against 'Magical Thinking': https://www.huffingtonpost.co.uk/entry/opinion-smith-obama-kin g_n_5a5903e0e4b04f3c55a252a4

20 Fuckers. https://www.theguardian.com/us-news/2022/jun/30/us-supreme-court-ruling-restricts-federal-power-greenhouse-gas-emissions

PIS ALLER

BY J.MCDONALD

I wipe my sweaty palms on my pants as I try to calm myself. I take deep breaths through my nose, flooding my system with the filtered oxygen that smells slightly of foliage and dampness. A year ago today I chose my name and began this next horrible step in my education.

I feel so much older. I remember being calm but excited when I woke up on that first day of my seventh year. I already knew what name I would choose to honour the lost – Geoclemys hamiltonii. I'd admired "turtles" and their slow cautious ways, but I'd also liked the idea of walking around with your own personal set of armour that doubled as a place to hide away from the world. Now, as I try once again to prepare myself for antiquities class, I long for the quiet safety of a shell.

When I glance to my right, I notice Perameles eremiana looking at me. I try to smile and decide there's no point. We both know that the majority of what awaits us inside the antiquities classroom is unpleasant. Our teacher, Trillium grandiflorum, says that we must begin with the macro and work our way down to the micro. Once we reach the micro there will be more enjoyable lessons. Unfortunately, as a species, it seems the majority of our ancestors' macro-level actions were… *upsetting*, to say the least. After a year of being immersed in the reconstructions of the past built by the elders, words like horrible, painful, and insane also spring to mind.

Our other classes, like geology, zoology, and botany, started with theory-based lessons, then moved to hands-on experiences. Antiquities, however, has been conducted in the holovision room from the beginning. Our teachers tell us that it's necessary to relive the mistakes of the past so that we can ensure we never repeat them ourselves.

I can't imagine ever being naïve or mean-spirited enough to come up with the majority of the barbarity I've witnessed in antiquities. Trillium says that this is because I've had the benefit of these lessons. In the past, antiquities was taught differently and the dry, data-focused methods of the past failed to demonstrate the mental, emotional, physical, and environmental impacts of our actions in a way that truly sank in for most people – leaving them susceptible to repeating the same mistakes over and over.

The doors to the classroom hiss as they open and Pera grabs my hand. I take comfort in the fact that I don't have to do this alone. We're never told ahead of time what the lesson will be. Since none of our lessons have been pleasant, I find myself trying to guess how awful today's experience will be on a scale of confusing to frightening.

The lights dim as the holovision takes over. I hear the crashing of waves and the floor begins to rock from side to side. Mist sprays my face. When I'm done wiping it away, the scene has fully loaded. We're on something I've learned is called a boat. The wooden boards beneath my feet are soaked in ocean water. Overhead, a Diomedeidae flaps its massive wings against a grey sky.

Seeing the sky is the only thing I enjoy about this room. It's been a long time since anyone has seen it. Not even the oldest inhabitants of *Pis Aller* can remember anyone who's been outside of the facility.

'Geo, can you tell me what century we're in?' Trillium looks at me expectantly.

I turn my focus back to the ship. It's made mostly of wood, which means trees were abundant, but the people weren't skilled enough yet to use metal or flora-fabricae.

'300 PE.' I try to sound confident in my answer but it's just a guess.

'Very close but we're actually a little earlier than that. The ship we're sailing aboard is a 400 PE whaling vessel. Can anyone tell me what that means? How about you, Felis jacobita?'

Felis looks around the deck and stares at the pronged and barbed instruments towards the bow. 'I'd say, given the equipment, they're not here for research and conservation.'

A few kids snicker at this, but I only feel sick at the thought of what those tools are used for. I realise Pera is still holding my hand when I feel a gentle squeeze.

Throughout the lesson, we never let go of each other. By the end, our hands are clasped so tightly that the pain almost distracts me from the haunting sight of the life draining from the whale's eye as it succumbs to the tortures it has endured. I finally let go when I run from the room to vomit.

*

That night, in the dining hall, I hear some of the elders discussing something called "The Leaving". I've heard rumours that our time in *Pis Aller* is almost up and we'll be free to move out into the world. Personally, I'm fine with *never* leaving. We have everything we need right here, and I've seen enough of the outside world in antiquities to last me a lifetime.

The elders chatting suddenly notice my curious gaze and go back to eating in silence. I try to turn my focus back to the conversation at my own table. Teacher Thaumoctopus mimicus is attempting to explain the Evacuation to some sixth years.

'The cataclysm didn't come from a single devastating natural disaster or age-ending meteor. It came on the back of billions of tiny decisions. A slow descent into madness.'

'What's that mean?' one of them asks. They remind me of a Micrathene whitneyi and I wonder if that's the name they will end up choosing for themselves.

'The catastrophes that led us here are not some judgement from a higher power or a vengeful planet out to eliminate a parasite from its surface. They were the logical consequence of an equation that is unbalanced. Some preferred to blame deities and prophecies for the travesties that were within their power to avoid the entire time.'

Another young one pipes up: 'I still don't get it.'

'Humans of the past valued convenience over conservation. For example, the napkin you're using is made from an old shirt that was too damaged to wear, so it was repurposed into several napkins, which will be washed and reused many times before they eventually need to be added to the compost. People of the past cut down trees, ground them, and made napkins that they would use once, then throw away. Their waste would go to a place called a dump that was too full of toxins and chemicals to make compost from. They did this because they were too lazy to wash the napkins or repurpose their resources.'

'But isn't that kind of like pooping your pants because you're too lazy to walk to the washroom?'

I couldn't help but laugh, water spurting painfully out of my nose.

'Yes, I suppose that is one way to look at it.' I could see Thaumo fighting the urge to smile too. 'The only problem is, in this case, the lazy person is not the only one to suffer.'

We're all quiet after that. The younger kids may not have faced the past in antiquities yet, but they've heard some of our stories. Images of wildfires, warzones, and oil spills flash before my eyes.

One of the little ones crosses their arms and pouts. 'It's not fair.'

'Fair or not, it's what happened. All we can do is try to fix what's been done.'

I've had enough of living in the past for one day. I clear my things from the table and prepare for bed.

*

Today's ecology lesson is thankfully focused on the present. Each year, we're given a deeper understanding of how the systems of *Pis Aller* work together to keep everyone alive. Unfortunately, it doesn't take long for Teacher Monodon monoceros to turn back to Earth and the past.

'Just like the planet, Pis Aller is both a closed loop and a living thing. The plants that cover the walls give us food just as we give them food. They filter our air and water and are nourished by the compost we give them. It is a never-ending cycle of giving. One cannot survive without the other. Many of our ancestors did not understand this relationship and they suffered for their ignorance.'

Suddenly Felis raises a hand but does not wait to be called on before speaking.

'Why are we spending so much time on what's already done and out of our control? Why aren't we preparing for The Leaving?'

Several of us gasp. There's always been an unspoken rule that the adults should never find out that we know about The Leaving – even though we don't really know anything at all. But now that the question is out there, we collectively hold our breaths as we wait for an answer.

'Well, Felis, it looks like some of us will be able to leave *Pis Aller* sooner than was originally thought possible. That is why we've been extending your lessons and increasing their frequency. This will be the first time since our ancestors built *Pis Aller* that anyone will have the means to journey beyond our walls.'

My eyes immediately dart to Pera's and they're as wide and shocked as mine must be. We've always been raised with the vague idea that people would eventually be able to leave, but it had never happened before. It was something that was always in the future – always.

Just then, the chime indicating shift change goes off and I swear Mono looks relieved. Everyone seems to be in shock as we gather our things to go to antiquities. As soon as we're out of the classroom, Felis turns to grab me by the shoulders.

'Can you believe this! This is going to be amazing. Just think of all the new flora and fauna we'll discover.'

My speechlessness doesn't dampen Felis' spirits. They continue rambling on about exploring while my brain darts from one terrifying antiquities lesson to the next. Nuclear plant meltdowns, desertification, mass flooding. *What if we just end up making the same horrible mistakes all over again? What if people forget everything we've learned?*

I'm not given much time to process this news. We arrive at the holovision room and are ushered in right away. The lights dim and I try to prepare myself for whatever's coming.

A warm dry breeze begins to swirl around the room. Some of us start coughing and sneezing. The air is full of dust that coats your throat. I pull my shirt up to cover my nose and mouth as the light is suddenly blazing down on us. The land is loose dust as far as the eye can see. It swirls in the air and shifts the surface of the ground. The breeze gradually picks up into a gale and we have to lean forward to keep from falling over with the force of it.

'Can anyone tell me when or where we might be today?' Trillium asks. It's hard to hear over the wind and our coughing. Trillium adjusts the calibration of the room to bring the gusts down to a more workable level.

After blinking some of the grit from my eyes, I spot rows and rows of dead Zea mays stalks. Pera has obviously noticed the same thing and answers Trillium's question.

'We're on a farm.'

'Correct. What else can you tell me?'

Pera looks around for more clues. In the distance, I see a large tilling machine and point it out.

'This farm is from the era when chemicals, instead of compost, were used to fertilize the soil because they overworked the land and didn't protect it from erosion.'

'Also correct. And how would we change things if we were the ones who needed to grow food?'

Felis pipes up this time, perhaps eager to show that they are ready to go out into the world for The Leaving.

'We would keep the ground covered, we would diversify the crops, and we wouldn't need such vast amounts of land because we'd have a solely plant-based diet. With no need for grazing pastures, animal feed crops, or feedlots, more of the land could be used for conservation.'

'Excellent, Felis!'

Felis seems eager to earn some extra praise and adds to the solution. 'We would also use our food scraps and feces to ensure the soil was well cared for.'

'Great job, Felis. Can anyone else tell me why these practices may be some of the most important changes humans could have made?'

In unison, the class chimes in, 'Because food production was one of the most destructive forces on the planet.'

Pleased with our progress, Trillium spends the remainder of our lesson flipping us around the Earth to show all the different ways in which farming the land and waters chipped away at the environment. By the end, I'm ready to skip dinner and head straight for my bunk, but Pera won't let me.

We grab some food and decide to take it to the gathering room. It's empty and peaceful in here since this room is reserved for meetings of the entire community. I find a spot behind one of the raised garden beds and plop down on the floor. Pera sits cross-legged with a wall of moss and ferns cushioning their back. We eat in comfortable silence. Pera's calm presence and the stillness of the room help to erase the stress of the day. I've just begun to doze off when the hiss of the door startles me awake.

The gathering room isn't off-limits, but I still feel like I've been caught breaking a rule. I peek out from behind the garden bed to see who has come in. A stream of older kids, maybe seventeenth or eighteenth-years, are taking seats along the benches facing the stage at the front of the room. They're followed by the council of elders who take their seats on the stage itself. Elder Nudibranchia stands to speak.

'As I'm sure you've heard, the time for The Leaving is quickly approaching. Those of you gathered here today will be the first to go.'

There are some murmurs and whispering in the audience and Nudibranchia gives them a minute to finish their discussions.

'I know that this is all very sudden, but you've been well

prepared. You've spent your entire lives training for this moment, and I have great respect for each and every one of you. The lessons given to you by your teachers have provided you with the tools you'll need to survive.'

Without even looking, I reach for Pera's hand. I can't believe this is happening. *How long will it be until we're forced to leave? Will they wait until we're older or is everyone going now?* I keep listening and hope there's a choice to stay behind.

Elder Nudibranchia takes a seat. It seems it's Elder Xiphias gladius's turn to speak.

'Today, we prepare you for your final lesson. This lesson will not be one that we teach you, but instead one that you teach the world. From here you must leave us. You must travel to the past and make them listen. Educate them and guide them away from destruction.'

Pera lets out a small gasp and I immediately cover my mouth to avoid doing the same. I glance at the older kids to see if they'd known about this, but they seem as surprised as we are. Some of them link their arms around each other.

'You'll be spread out across different nations and different time periods. You'll go in teams of two or three so that you're not completely alone and you'll be given contacts who will be likely to help you when you arrive. These people were either known for their kindness or were advocates for the environment.'

Some of the people in the audience begin to cry, some look angry, and others just sit there staring straight ahead. Pera and I turn to each other. Neither of us seems able to find the words to describe our shock and dread at what we've just heard. All I can do is hold Pera tight.

Elder Scarabaeidae rises and the room falls silent.

An eighteenth-year also stands and waits. Scarabaeidae nods in their direction but starts to speak.

'I'm sure you have many questions and we will get to those in a moment. First, we would like to give you an explanation.'

Elder Xiphias stands once again and approaches the front of the stage. 'When our colony was created, it was the last hope of humanity but it was never expected to be a solution – more like a stalling tactic. The greatest minds of the time gathered to work towards the goal we recently achieved, the only thing that could possibly save the Earth – the ability to go back and undo the irreparable damage we'd done as a species.'

Unable to stay quiet any longer, the standing eighteenth-year speaks out: 'Why do we have to go at all? Why can't we let the past be the past and worry about what can be done now?'

Elder Nudibranchia leaves the stage. They walk over and place their hands on the shoulders of the older student. 'Bambusoideae, the truth is, there is nothing left to save. The Earth has been devoid of life for centuries, with no signs of recovery.'

Elder Xiphias continues with the explanation they had started. 'Our ancestors gathered as many resources as they could and, throughout the time our people have spent here, we've made good use of what we have. But, frankly, we're running out of essential materials. Things like our lighting system rely on metals and gases that were mined from the planet. We don't have the ability to reproduce them and, without the lights, we cannot adequately feed the plants which clean our air and water, and provide our food.'

The crowd murmurs and Pera and I look at each other. I feel a tear trickle down my cheek as I realise we won't be able to stay, but Pera looks strangely calm. I imagine that I can see gears spinning in Pera's head. They've done the calculations, accepted the facts, and are ready to face what's next. Pera's acceptance makes me want to cry even more. I want to fight this but my attention is drawn back to the stage.

Elder Nudibranchia is speaking again. 'Your age group has been chosen as the first to go. You're old enough and have adequate training to fend for yourselves, but you're also young enough that you have a better chance of surviving in the eras you'll be placed in. To have as great an impact as possible, our entire community will be spread across time in the hopes that each of our small ripples can form a wave.'

The conversation continues but I'm not able to focus anymore. Everyone, every single person I've known, is going to be ripped away. We'll be forced to live the rest of our lives in the real-life tortures of the antiquities room.

I don't notice that I'm shaking until I feel Pera's arms around me. 'Geo, it will be alright. We'll go together and we'll make the biggest difference out of anyone. We'll work with animals that have been dead for centuries. We'll feel the sun on our skin. We'll show them how to appreciate and care for what they have.'

Knowing what I do from our lessons, I'm not as optimistic, but I have to hope that Pera is right. If we can't make them listen, then we're all doomed.

THE MOUSE

BY NADINE DALTON-WEST

We are going to see the mouse! Daddy promised on my birthday – my ninth birthday, which was a long time ago, because now I am nine and a half – that we would go to see the mouse. I didn't believe him at all. Tickets are very hard to get, and the queues are very long, almost as long as bread queues or queues for cooling pods, but last week he came home and picked me up and twirled me right around, like he used to when I was a little girl, and said, "Ariadna, we are really, truly, actually going to see the mouse!" And I squealed as I went around, and Mummy did one of her serious looks and said, "We will discuss this later," and Daddy and I laughed because that almost always means that he is in Trouble-with-a-capital-T.

I think Mummy was upset because seeing the mouse is hard. She thinks it will be Too Much and Too Far and Too Risky, especially for a little girl. Sometimes I tell her that she is understandably struggling with me growing up, and she gives me a serious look. I try to sympathise with her. Things are not like they were when she was little, I tell her. The telecasts all say we are in the Far-Modern World now, and that we have to adapt, acclimatise and adjust. I like that saying because of all the A-words which make me feel as though my name should be on the end of it: adapt, acclimatise and adjust, Ariadna. I have adopted it as my motto, and would make it into a badge if I still had my badge machine. I still make tiny drawings of it in crayon, and cut them into circles, and put them next to my badges of animals on my pinboard.

(These are my animal badges that I have made so far: triceratops, minotaur, hippopotamus, panda, kakapo, phoenix, monkey, domestic feline felix felix, bumble bee. I arrange them into sections based on if they are extinct or mythical. Domestic feline felix felix is a difficult one. On the telecasts they call them "rumoured extinct pending confirmation," which makes them not like the others. And in my opinion, they are still alive but they live in the woods and in cold places like Canada, like Mummy and Daddy's felix, Cody. They still have pictures of him from before owning domestic animals was illegal, ages before I was born. He made his way to a boat and went to live in the woods, they say, so others must have done it too.)

Well my badge machine, which used to ther-CHUNK my pictures into actual badges with pins on, had to be given to the last metal collection, when everyone had midnight street parties to celebrate giving precious things back to the government, and we made bunting in the shape of cutlery and lamps and bicycles. So now I just make the pictures.

When they announced on the telecast that the mouse was coming back, I wore out my brown and grey and white crayons making pictures of mice. I might be an artist when I grow up. I have a signature ready and everything. Unfortunately, I made so many mouse pictures, my e-teacher had to have a word with Mummy. They are much more strict about drawing in Year 5.

All of this is why – because Mummy is having a serious

word with Daddy, and because our electricity session is in the mornings right now, so I can't even put on some songs and dance around to ignore them – I am writing in my diary that we are going to see the mouse!

*

We are going to see the mouse! Only today we are really going, and so we wake up in the middle of the night, and Mummy packs us lunches in wax wrappers and Daddy fusses about hoods and cool packs for the train, and then Daddy and I tiptoe down the staircase and out into the bluey-black night-time. I have planned everything and written it down for us, in my best handwriting.

1. Walk from our apartments to the Night Tram (20 mins)
2. Take the Night Tram to the Train Station (30 mins)
3. Wait for health testing and BioID security at Train Station (could be an hour, they do not like to say)
4. Take the Night Train to New Oxford (3 hours but allow for interrupted power supply, terror events, protests on the line, unexpected rail expansion events and other disruptions to your journey)
5. Walk from New Oxford Station to Old Oxford Town

The last one was very hard to find out information about because, like with the laboratory and BioZoo compound, they do not like to make the details available on the internet. I have decided to make notes about each one in turn, so I remember everything. I have decided I may want to be an Investigative Journalist when I grow up. I practise saying "Ariadna Davidson, EBC Telecasts, Milton Keynes," till Daddy asks me to stop it.

1. Everything is very dark blue with lots of tiny lights. Lots of people are awake to enjoy the cool hours. On

the streets it is quiet, with just the noise of far-away voices, the wind and the ticking noise of people's roof turbines. The streets are very wide and long and empty. The lamp posts glitter softly with bluey-green solar lights.

2. The Night Tram stop is very bright! Daddy says Vital Infrastructure has electricity all the time. It makes my eyes squint. The Night Tram arrives and makes a very nice swooshing noise, and thirteen people get on board at our stop. The dark buildings and tiny lights all blur as we swoosh past them.

3. I hardly cry at all at the blood testing! Daddy says he is extremely proud of me. The fingertip one for BioID is not so bad, but the syringe one for disease testing is horrible. The needle goes very deep. I look in the opposite direction into the big lights and count signs. These are the ones I see: wear your filtration hood; are YOU concealing vital metals; curfew is safer for us ALL; public drunkenness – the shame of taking more than your share; report water use violations HERE. By the time I have read them all, the needle has stopped.

4. We have permission to travel and we have no known diseases! We are allowed onto the Night Train. Daddy holds my hand and we go down more steps and wait on a long, long platform. The train is not swooshy like the tram – it is really loud and the metal screams on other metal and fills your head with noise. The seats are big and made of velvet material, and Daddy lets me sit by the window. I have brought a book to read, of course, and my colouring crayons, but I stare out of the window for a long time. After the station, we go into blackness for a while – high black shadows and little pin-prick lights like stars again, which means we are still

in the town. Then lots of lights again at a checkpoint, where we stop for a minute. Then blackness, then more lights. The train driver brings up shutters after a while, because we are passing through the refugee zones, and I write my investigative journalist observations and do some drawings of the people I have seen so far tonight. By the time he brings the shutters down again, the blackness is turning blue and grey, and I watch the light slowly change the colours of the horizon.

5. New Oxford Station is very much more scary than I had expected. After about an hour or so, the Night Train slows down and then stops, and outside the windows in the soft blue you can see a high wall of wire that goes on forever, on either side of the train and higher than the train roof – much higher, with coiled spring wire on the very top. There are men with guns and air-hoods who board the train, and men outside who sweep scanning sticks across it, and other clunks and bangs all around it, and something that sounds like gunfire, until even I get a bit scared and have to cuddle Daddy for a bit. He whispers to me that crossing into New Oxford is one of the most difficult crossings in the whole world now. When the train is allowed forward and very slowly pulls up at a long grey platform, we get out very carefully and very slowly. Outside, I look up and it is amazing. The Biodomes of New Oxford glow like gold as the sun comes up.

*

We are going to see the Mouse! We have to wear our permission badges now, outside of our clothes, and our papers are checked again before they let us out of the huge concrete tunnel and into the early dawn light. I hold Daddy's hand because there are so many people, some from the train, some from other places, and we walk and walk. We are on a moving walkway but it is still very far. The air here smells different from the air in London. In Year 4 our e-class did a project on it and learned all of the important science and history, and I know why: the air in London is air, so it smells and has dirt in it, and if you go outside for too long your snot goes black and your hair gets gritty. But the air in New Oxford is all filtered and treated, every bit of it, and in the hottest times it is even temperature-treated so that everything is cool and fresh underneath the Biodome. This is because New Oxford is the place where the most important people in the world live. As we walk along the metal walkway which makes a gentle hissing noise, we start to see lots of buildings on either side of us. I grab Daddy's arm.

'Look, Daddy,' I say. I point with my notepad and pencil. I might be a tour guide when I grow up. 'The wide building with green glass walls is the House of Parliament.'

'Mmmm,' he says.

'And the tall one with blue glass is the Citadel.'

'Ah,' he says.

'And the really tall one on the left with the spikes is the Palace.'

'Really?' he asks, but I feel like he does not mean it. I could tell him all about the temporary members who live in the Parliament, and the permanent members who live in the Citadel, and about the war between them, and about poor mad King Louis the Third who lives in the palace and is one hundred and twelve years old and has a bionic eyeball, but I don't think he is listening. He is staring at the buildings ahead of us instead.

'Oxford,' he says. His tone is funny.

'OLD Oxford,' I remind him.

He looks down at me, and then back up again.

The buildings ahead are where the walkway stops. They are half there and half not, because they were badly burned and bombed during the second resource war. 'The Bodleian,' Daddy murmurs, and this time he is the one who points, and I look. It is a low, green, metal dome inside a sky-high bio-dome, held up on scaffolding, with a half-stone circle and a half-metal circle underneath.

But it is not what Daddy said now, not at all. It is the entrance to the BioZoo.

*

We are here, right here, to see the Mouse!

The crowd is growing now. There is a low, excited muttering. Everyone is excited but quiet, and as you pass underneath the old dome and down the escalator to the underground complex, it feels like going into somewhere magical. Everything is cool, and the lights are light purple and white, and there are high, high ceilings and walls of glass and a sound of running water. We pass through an archway that hisses at us, and looks like the whale jawbones from the history books, but the teeth are nozzles and the hissing is a sterilising mist. One day, maybe a thousand years ago, a whale and a mouse might have seen each other, one on a cliff top and one in the sea, and I am about to tell Daddy when the walls turn more purple and a booming starts. Music.

'Decades ago,' says a voice, and we all swivel our heads around but there is no sign of a man, or of speakers, 'the Zoological Archive Museum began its pioneering work to catalogue and preserve the irreplaceable species that humankind was losing to the epidemic of…'

'Look, Daddy,' I say, and point. On the purple walls, all around us, a telecast is playing. Animals pour down the walls, hundreds of them, more than I have in my badge collection. They are the dead ones. Kakapo. Bumble Bee. Felix felix.

'It was in this spirit,' continues the voice, 'that our farsighted founders broke ground on the Revivification Centre. To let there be life!'

The walls are doors. They slide open suddenly, where there was no join and no door. We shuffle, silently now, into a space in front of a glass wall. Behind it are men and women in white coats and hoods, walls of what look like cages, and silver machines all around. And maybe this is where all of our metals go, because there are metals everywhere, dry-looking and with a dull shine. In front of them, a separate room with glass walls, and a glass door.

And a pod; a pod like a huge egg in the middle of a white, white floor.

A whooshing sound. The door into the glass room slides open, and then closed. One of the scientists steps forwards.

'You join us now at a remarkable point in our journey,' he says, and the shuffling crowd make an 'oooohhh' sound that stays in the room and echoes. Behind him, something strange is happening. The other white coats are moving, making little clusters, holding their ears. Someone points. The talking man does not stop. 'Our first mouse – mus musculus – died in the incubation chamber ten years ago. Our second lived a short while, and our third and fourth were weeks old when they expired, every one a blueprint for our next attempt at revivification. Every one teaching us to select for strength, size, resilience in the DNA.'

I start to pull at Daddy's arm. 'Daddy,' I say, and he taps me and shushes me, but the white coats behind the man are trying to get his attention now. I think something has happened.

'And now,' the man says, and his voice echoes through the

speakers and stays. 'The presentation of Mouse 25: the final proof that humankind can shake off the tragedies of mass extinction and bring our biodiversity back in glorious resurrection!'

Loud music, very loud, happens.

The pod cracks. It opens. We see the mouse.

It is brown, and it is sitting still. It is big. It is much bigger than my drawings, much bigger than in the books I have by my bed. Bigger even than a rat. It sits up on its hindquarters and sniffs, and you can see it has a white belly, pink nose, pink, oval ears that twitch and move. Its black, shining eyes are beautiful. Slowly, it turns its head.

The music stops. The scientist man steps towards the mouse and opens his mouth to speak.

When the mouse crouches, and jumps, and flies through the air, it is completely silent. Then there is a scream that stops and becomes a wet, awful sound, because the mouse has torn open the man's throat, and bright red, red like paint, splatters the inside of the glass, and the screaming is now on our side of the glass, and it is rising. I look up at daddy and his face is pale, and he drops his hands to try to cover my eyes and ears. His hands are hot and they hurt. I squeeze my own eyes closed and put my hands up, and then he is picking me up and lifting me and pressing me into his body, turning my face away from the glass and over his shoulder, and he starts running.

When I peek behind us, as he runs with me in his arms and we run back, back towards the long corridor, where there are alarms and flashing red lights now, not animal pictures and purple softness, I can see these things.

1. There are hundreds of us, all running.
2. The man's body is on the floor.
3. The wooshing door behind him is open, and there are more people, and more blood, and cages, cages with their doors hanging open.

4. The glass window we were standing next to, only a minute ago. The glass window is cracking.

*

On the train, we are very quiet. When we look at the news-screens, they are filled with pictures of the Prime Minister meeting the leader of the Free North in the capital, outside York Minster. They are shaking hands and smiling. There is nothing at all about New Oxford, or about what has happened. Nothing about scientists and blood. Nothing about hundreds of people getting to the train station just before they shut the city and the biodome down.

Daddy lost our bag. He left it behind when we were running. At the station, he buys two sandwiches in blue wax papers, and in the quiet of the train he slides one across the table towards me. His fingers are shaking.

'Daddy?' I say.

'Mmmm.'

'What will happen?'

'I don't know,' he says. He stares out of the window for a long time, at the setting sun. His face is golden and he looks old.

'Why did the mice hate the men?'

He stares some more, and then turns his head away from the window toward me. His eyes are shining and wet.

'Perhaps they always did,' he says.

I push my sandwich away and sit very still. The air is very cool and dry. I do not want to be a reporter anymore. I do not want to think about what I can't stop thinking about, about what if the mice get outside the biodome, and about what is happening to the people who are still inside.

I think about my badges, hundreds of them, made of paper and metal, and how I will change them. I will have to make them so much bigger, and give them sharp teeth.

Or maybe I do not want them after all, now.

Now that I have really seen the mouse.

SNOWGLOBED

BY MARK KIRKBRIDE

Jim settled into the high-backed mesh chair and swivelled to pass the last seconds before they went on air. The chair squeaked. Misaligned with his microphone, he froze.

'Going live in five,' began the producer in the cans over his ears. 'Three, two, one, and…'

All Jim could make out of his friend Bob Sterring, the show's presenter, seated opposite, was a large red microphone and a greying fringe.

'Thank you, Carol,' intoned Bob. 'Well, I'm very pleased to have in the studio today someone that everyone at DBCK Radio will know very well… Jim Frante.'

'Hello, Bob.' Zigzagged in his chair, Jim addressed the microphone Anglepoised towards his ear. 'It's good to be back.'

'So, Jim, how goes the crusade?'

Jim leaned back in the chair, which tilted alarmingly. He leaned forwards and his shoes clunked to the floor. He twisted back towards the microphone. 'Well, Bob, I wouldn't call it a crusade exactly…'

Bob laughed. 'Well, a cause then, Jim.'

'Hm, OK, *maybe*,' said Jim. 'But more like an appeal. An appeal for common sense, Bob. Everyone's going on about climate change like it's a *thing*. Like it's something to be afraid of, something to be worried about, something to feel *guilty* about.'

'Then what can you say to reassure them, Jim?' asked Bob, in his most sonorous radio voice.

Jim's chair shifted to the left and back. He gripped the armrests, clinging on. 'It's natural is all I'm saying, Bob. Little Ice Ages have happened before. We had one starting in the 1300s. The Thames used to freeze over. Between the 1600s and the 1800s, frost fairs took place on the river. I remember studying it at school.' He enjoyed dropping in the odd ad-lib but that was a genuine memory. 'The present cooling is all part of those same natural cycles,' he continued. 'Storms, heavy snow, ports locked in by ice – all perfectly normal. It's just the timings and the extent that changes. And there are any number of possible causes, not least volcanic activity or fluctuations in solar radiation.' He cleared his throat. 'Plus there will always be winners and losers in these things. We don't have to flagellate ourselves when it should all just even itself out. We need to hold our nerve and take the long view.'

'So what would you say to those who are calling for drastic action?'

Jim's jaw clicked. 'Well, what would be catastrophic would be to decimate entire industries on which our economy depends to counteract something that is, as I say, strictly natural. We can beat ourselves up as much as we like but we've just got to ride it out.'

'So what would your message be to anyone out there who's really feeling the chill right now?'

Jim smiled – though this was completely lost on a radio show, he realised (apart from the hardcore webcam audience).

'It's simple, Bob. So it's a little cold out there? *Well, put a jumper on.*'

Bob laughed. '"Put a jumper on." Love it. Pithy as ever, Jim.'

'Well, I try, Bob. I try.'

'Thank you – Jim Frante.'

'A pleasure, Bob. A pleasure as always.'

'Well, after the break we'll be talking to Labour MP Marcus Rashford about the legacy of the Corbyn government, and no doubt asking whether England can repeat their 2021 World Cup win...'

Jim took his headphones off, waited for the signal from the producer, and slipped out of the studio. His assistant Anaya, in a Mesh & Cope jacket and Storm boots, met him outside. They retrieved his Toppel coat from the green room and he picked up the coffee he hadn't had time to touch.

He glanced at straight-backed Anaya as they stopped out in the corridor. 'OK, how long have we got?'

With her tablet clamped under her elbow, she consulted her watch. 'We should be hitting the road now. You're on air at BBX in an hour.'

'OK, so let's go.' He sniffed as they turned up the corridor. 'What will the next one be like?'

'Oh, that was a walk in the park compared to the next one.'

'Ah.'

Back on the ground floor, they crossed the foyer. Beyond the floor-to-ceiling window, snow billowed and roiled. Old drifts lay heaped against the front of the building in cross-section. They passed through one set of glass doors, then the next. The cold smacked him. He did up the last 'V' of his coat with trembling hands and stiffening fingers.

Spilling coffee on the cleared path, he slipped. 'Whoa...'

'You alright?' A hand at his back supported him.

'Yeah, careful, that's black ice.'

Numb lips failed to form around the words. Puffing cloud-breaths, they crossed the concourse. The 4x4 purred at the kerb and in a moment its warmth enveloped them.

*

'So what you're saying is that we're all overreacting and that we should just sit back and wait for it to pass?' pressed Ann Driebs, of Action Against Extreme Freezing.

She wore arctic combat fatigues and a high-viz green jacket. Did she want to be seen or not?

Jim opened his mouth, hesitated. Was it a trap? He couldn't leave dead air, the ultimate *faux pas* on radio. 'Basically, yes.'

'While whole countries grind to a halt and people literally freeze to death?'

Why didn't Pippy Quinterton, the host, step in? Jim peered across at her, trying to catch her eye, then glanced round as a man who'd joined them in the tiny studio took the seat and yellow microphone next to his.

Jim leaned towards his blue mike. 'Well, I…'

'What are you gonna tell us to do,' Ann interrupted, '"put a jumper on"?'

Jim swallowed. That catchphrase had worn out quickly. He'd have to find another one.

'You could try a coat,' he quipped.

'What, indoors?' sneered Ann. 'I'm just curious… Is this what you believe or what you're paid to say?'

'This is my job.'

'And this is mine,' Ann stated. 'Unpaid.'

'Alright, alright,' Pippy cut in, a bit late. 'So, final thoughts, please, the two of you. We have just thirty seconds left. Ann… you first.'

'Global freezing is happening, global freezing is real, and we need to do something about it, now.' Ann swung her gaze from Pippy to him. 'We need to cut emissions and stop choking the atmosphere, let the heat of the sun heal our wintered planet.'

'And Jim,' cued Pippy. 'Just time for a quick response on that.'

'I agree. I agree with Ann. It is man-made.' He let the dead air hang as the producer counted down with his fingers at the window. 'A man-made myth!'

Ann's head jerked towards her microphone.

Pippy raised a palm. 'OK, thank you, Ann Driebs. Thank you, Jim Frante.' The other man at the table shuffled his papers. 'Time for a round-up of the news now but join us in a few minutes when we'll be talking to European Union expert Jake Kreeson, the author of a new book asking, what if Brexit had actually happened? How much richer would we all be?'

*

Jim sat in the back next to Anaya as skein upon skein of whiteness flung itself at the SUV and eddied around it, the car slithering and yawing on the white roads.

He brushed snow off his coat. 'OK, so what's up next?'

Anaya tapped her tablet, scrolled. 'Oliver has you pitched against an environmental activist. A schoolgirl.'

'A schoolgirl…?'

Anaya scrolled a little more. 'Well, she used to be a schoolgirl.'

Jim laughed. 'Everybody used to be a schoolgirl, or a schoolboy.'

'Well, this one's getting very hot under the collar about it getting very cold in Sweden.'

Jim squinted at her. 'Isn't it supposed to be cold in Sweden? Can't we get her a blankie or something?'

'Oliver's not given her name but it's Greta something or other…'

Jim took a sip of his latest coffee. It had gone cold. He placed the cup in the holder. 'Rings a bell. We may have had a Twitter spat.'

'Very articulate and controlled but lets her emotions show to devastating effect. It's really important this one goes well.' Anaya checked her watch. 'Plus it's live TV, so we can't be late.'

Jim leaned forwards. 'Frank, how's it looking?'

'It's not, Mr Frante,' replied the driver. 'Can barely see a thing.'

Ahead, behind, whiteout. Front and back, wipers no sooner swiped falling snow out of the way than another layer of feathery flakes connected with those already adhering. Jim compared the right to the left: the outline of buildings, lightly etched; the white wind in between. The snow made each gust manifest. Very little traffic passed the other way. Everyone had heeded the warnings about the latest arctic storm.

'Where are we?' Jim demanded.

'We've just gotta get round the park, then we'll be there.'

Gradually, the buildings dropped away to the left and a white desert stretched off to that side. They passed a stationary bus: dark inside, white on the outside. The wind howled around the 4x4, which rocked on its axis, one way, the other. What was that? Rucks in the ice? Something scraped the underside of the vehicle, which didn't sound good. Then the front end went up, with a shushing sound followed by a creak as they came to a halt.

'What…' Jim turned to Anaya. 'Are you okay?'

'Yes,' she managed, half sitting, half lying now.

Frank hung above them.

'Frank, Frank, what happened?' Jim wanted to know.

Frank's eyes met his in the rear-view mirror. 'Sorry, Mr Frante. I think we hit a drift.'

The driver put the 4x4 into reverse, forward. Forward, reverse. They tilted each time. Snow fountained ahead, behind, beyond the frantic wipers.

'Great, an SUV that can't manage roads,' thought Jim.

Frank craned around. 'I could try and dig us out, Mr Frante.'

'No, no, no, there isn't time. Listen, you phone ahead, Anaya, and call for a pick-up truck.' They came with snowploughs these days, didn't they? 'I'm gonna head across the park. The studio's just over there, right, Frank?'

Anaya touched his arm. 'Jim – Mr Frante – no.'

Jim pushed at the hatch of the door. Cold whipped around him and he almost regretted the decision but he couldn't turn back now. He dropped to the ground, up to his shins in snow. The cold instantly started biting at him. Lights had come on. The lampposts illuminated fat grey flakes like moths. Crooked shadows fell across lumpy ground. The wind whistled. All across the park, white drapes closed from left to right upon white drapes closing from left to right. On and on they went, closing, closing, closing, in endless recession.

'It's Storm Henry,' he shouted. 'How bad can Storm Henry be?'

*

He'd found an entrance and he could see lights coming on one by one on the other side of the park. It couldn't be that far. He could hear Anaya's shouts recede into the distance behind him with every tread, or thought he could.

Snow lay heaped in every direction. He leaned into icy sideswipes of wind that, scooping and sculpting, rearranged the white dunes in endless susurrations. Fresh flakes stung his face. New powdery snow creaked with each ponderous step. Sometimes his foot sank further, crunching through underlayers, and he swayed but the snow was so deep that it propped him up.

He only had shoes on, not boots. Each time he lifted a foot out, snow caked his trousers. One side of his coat had turned white. The mini-tusk of an icicle hung from his left nostril. More ice caked his eyebrows. He pictured them, white against his scorched face. He'd stuffed his raw, clawed, useless hands far inside his pockets as he held his upper body rigid against the flesh-withering wind.

'What am I doing?' he thought.

He stopped.

Like a man in a snowglobe that had been given a violent shake, he stood there as flakes surged and swirled all around him.

Was he doing the right thing? Should he admit defeat, turn back?

Glancing behind him, he couldn't even see the Sevarro anymore.

No, he couldn't let a bit of snow, or a schoolgirl, beat him. He trudged deeper and deeper into the petrified park as the white storm raged around him.

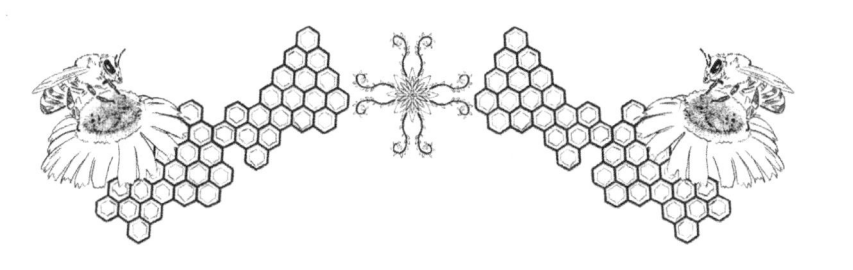

CHARLI

BY JOHN J ERNEST

I start my day like most folks, attacked by a flock of chickens while trying to fix pump six in agriculture hangar four. I swear, if Stevenson doesn't maintain those pumps better, we're going to lose more than twenty litres of H_2O next time they break down. And why, dear god why, do they have so many chickens loose in that hangar?

Anyway, that's where I am when I get the call. Heidi from management buzzes through, asking if I'm on duty for the dome. Well, seeing as we don't have a specific rota for dome maintenance, I say I'm on emergency repairs duty, which is close enough.

Forty-five minutes later I'm stood under the main dome, staring up with a crick in my neck from laying under a hydration unit all morning. I scrutinise the dome, looking for any possible issues while waiting on Heidi, and Malcolm, the senior engineer, to tell me what the ruckus is all about.

Malcolm wheels himself in, he has that smile on his face, I remember it from when we were kids, he just loves a challenge, and his enthusiasm is infectious. It got us in a lot of trouble as kids.

I can't help but wonder why he hasn't gone for a support suit; stubborn bastard is still using a manual chair when he could be walking around. Whenever I mention it, he just says the tech is better used on the young: like we're that old? It's an argument we've had for many years: he brings up the shortage of materials, and I bring up how important it is for him to get around. He's yet to convince me and I'm yet to get out of it without a hangover.

I give him a smile as he hands me a coffee, which seems like a fair trade. We both wait there another five minutes, neither breaking the silence as we sip the coffee. The only sound is the low hum of the pumps along the base of the dome. There aren't many people I'm comfortable with. Malcolm is top of the list, but I wouldn't tell him that.

We both turn as Heidi saunters out of the office, as if she wasn't the one panicking on the coms earlier. She looks up, and we wait a minute or so before she asks if we know where sector forty-two is.

We both look at her like she's speaking Martian. It's an in-joke for the engineers, we're not allowed to explain it. Anyway, after staring back up at the dome for a minute, and counting in our heads, we point at the same section, right near the top. She passes me a scope and asks me to view it, some kid stargazing last night reported a crack in the dome. She needed to know the severity of it before allocating resources.

Malcolm laughs while reaching over the back of his chair for an antique pair of binoculars. I mean these things predate the hab project by at least fifty years. His fascination with old tech is entertaining enough, but where does he keep finding the stuff?

Anyway, we both stare up at the dome. Malcolm's fiddling around with his binoculars while my scope autofocuses and tells me the range. Two hundred and twenty-five feet at its apex. I geotag it, and it gives me the temperature at target; even through the multi-layered glass and steel it's thirty-six degrees up at the top.

The main dome is a beaut. Solar panels attached to the external steel supports, a water system integrated into the lower glass shelves providing essential UV protection, light, power, and heating to everything in habs two and three, which were originally just one hab unit back at the start of the project.

I tell Heidi, while scouring the panel, that there hasn't been a crack in this glass for a hundred years; it's the original, and, in my opinion the best design of the time.

Then I see it, right where the kid said, section forty-two, second ring of panels out from the centre, fourth panel round. The panels have a cleaning process, air wash to remove dust and particulates, my first thought goes to debris, but with my own two eyes I see the shadow of a big black line, maybe an arm's length, near the edge of that panel.

In minutes I'm on to Stevenson, he needs to prep an EVA suit and fuel up Bessie. I can make it to the garage in thirty minutes. Malcolm is on his pad checking the forecast, no storms today, that's a relief. Last thing I need is to be climbing over two hundred feet up, suited and hauling a resin gun while dealing with a sandstorm.

Just between us, I'm scared, I haven't been up on a dome in a while, and no one goes outside unless it's absolutely necessary. I'm thinking worst case scenarios; if it's a multi-layer crack the resin won't cut it, can't just seal it and pray. Not like the other habs with their thicker glass and fewer layers. If we lose functionality of dome three, the filtration for most of our agriculture hangars goes down. That's food we can't waste. Plants that replenish our oxygen, filter water, hell, even keep those damn chickens around.

So, I'm thinking we can plate that panel, I'm already doing the math in my head, where we can scavenge some plate from, how much weld would be needed, the best sealant for the job, how many of us to winch it up, totally lost in thinking my way around the problem.

Before I know it, I'm sat in the back of Bessie, staring at the ugliest EVA suit you've ever seen. Bessie is a repurposed lunar rover. Huge tyres, massive ride height, sealed driver's compartment, and a large passenger and cargo area. I'm sat there, while Stevenson is spraying the suit; get this: with old-school deodorant. Like that's going to change the fact these suits are rarely cleaned. I give him the stink-eye, he knows I'm reporting this. Suit maintenance is his jurisdiction, and I'm about to climb into quite possibly the most disgusting stench ever.

Malcolm is hauling himself into the driver's seat and Stevenson hightails it out of the garage, sealing it behind as I'm climbing into the suit, trying not to breathe through my nose. Once I'm in, helmet sealed, I bang on the wall and Malcolm turns the UV screen up. He drives her out quick as a whip, as soon as the bay doors are open, I swear he didn't even wait for the second doors to finish rolling up.

Malcolm is an odd fish, he's all holier than though when discussing schematics, system improvements, water cycling and the like, he knows his stuff, possibly the smartest guy in the room. Then you get him behind the wheel, and he's sixteen again, in the corridor karts, rattling along the lower hangars. Banging into geo-piping, overriding speed limiters, jumping thermal vents, causing his dad all manner of problems.

Needless to say, we have a bit of fun before we get outside dome three. Malcolm has me screaming and laughing like a kid again, hanging on as he throws Bessie's rear end around the bends. Takes my mind right off the climb. I think that's his intention, like I said, he's a smart one that Malcolm.

So, I'm in the suit, smelling every engineer or tech that went outside to get samples or whatnot over the last year, and trying not to think about it. Bessie is parked to give me some shade at the base of the support. Malcolm knows when I need mic chatter and when I don't, he's thankfully quiet as I stare up at the long climb.

I strap the resin gun to my back and clip myself into the cable running up the side of the support. I can feel the heat from the steel even through the thick gloves. A few deep breaths and then, like Sisyphus, I put one foot in front of the other and make my way up that dome. What, you think just because we live underground, we can't learn Greek mythology?

I get to about a hundred feet, the supports all look good, a bit sand-beaten and smoothed in places, the winds sure did pick up over the past few decades. I turn to look out over the desert. Even through the suit's visors the sun is blinding, I'm not going to say like a hammer on an anvil, because what with the thin atmosphere and the lack of oxygenating plants, this planet is just damn inhospitable, it doesn't need me adding insult to injury by throwing clichés into the mix.

I buzz through to Malcolm, in my sweetest voice, and mention that I really should have gone to the bathroom before I climbed up. He laughs, I laugh, and I take in the view a bit more.

It's beautiful, you know, like those cats I've read about that used to live in Africa, deadly, but so damn beautiful. Every time I go out dayside I am in awe of its beauty, so many shades of red, orange, and yellow. A desert, sure, but it's got depth, history, colour. I climb another thirty feet before I take my next break. Starting to feel the heat now. I realise I'm starting to stink just as bad as the suit, maybe I should recommend getting Stevenson an apprentice, to help with his maintenance chores.

The inner lining of the suit sticks to the skin, it chafes at the chest. I buzz down to Malcolm and ask when the next bath is free on the rota. A shower just isn't going to cut it after this.

While I wait for a reply, and catch my breath, I turn again, looking out at the bay. We call it the bay, but the sea hasn't been here for a long time. I can see black dots out in the valley, the old sea floor. Antique ships, now brittle and useless, beaten daily by the insane amounts of radiation raining down from above, nothing more than piles of rust waiting to collapse in on themselves.

Then it catches my eye, a line of deep crimson pointing up towards the sky, the last remnants of the gate, the old bridge that crossed the sea. Man, I would have loved to have seen so much water in one place, so big you needed boats and bridges to cross it. I made a note to myself to head down to the reservoir, spend some time in the dark and enjoy the sound of the water. I'm assured that there are still some large bodies of water out there, although most are now subterranean, or vapour farms around the equator.

The gate fell before I was born, some terrorist act or something, a disenfranchised faction of society rebelling against the Mars programme, no one was ever caught, they all had bigger issues to deal with. It was just before the gate fell that the near-light engine was discovered, the big rush followed, and humanity either went under the earth or out into the void, like rats abandoning ship.

As I turn to resume the climb I notice the pipework for the air cleaning, it's beaten and decayed. This section must have been constructed from substandard materials. I make a note to add it to the list of things to repair. It might be why the crack formed: if the pressure higher up was affected, the panels above wouldn't be kept clear of sand and debris. I buzz down to Malcolm, give him the news that the area below forty-two needs air pipes replacing. He uses some of his more colourful swear words.

I laugh and carry on up, with each step I think about the last hundred or so years of history, how we'd tried to reverse the damage, then tried to adapt to it, or just gave up and left.

I recently read about that guy, Kamachi I think his name was, he tried to alter rice so it could survive the new levels of UV and other aberrant radiation. His strain worked for a while, but eventually became inedible, even poisonous. Most of us accepted our new lives, we made leaps in subterranean food growth, geothermal energy supply, water cycling. A mostly vegetarian diet and oxygen recycling, it all helped keep us clinging on. I don't know who said it, might be a misremembered quote, "calamity breeds ingenuity". I will have to look up where that's from, maybe get it put up in the workshop.

By the time I reach sector forty-two I'm knackered, put a fork in me, done. This here was my exercise for a month. I tie myself to a support and lean against the dome for five minutes. I take one more look around at the barren seabed, and a sky so crystal clear, it looks like new glass; we haven't seen clouds North of the tropics in a lifetime. Once I get my breath, I turn to fix the crack, luckily for me I can now see the dark line clearly, about ten feet away, just above a smaller support. So, I feed out more cable and inch my way towards it.

Sliding my feet, less than a foot at a time, I creep closer and closer, my mind playing havoc with me. What if the support buckled? What if the dome gave way? What if I can't fill the crack with resin? Plating it would only be a short-term fix. We could salvage glass panels from the old military station in the south, but that's a trip and a half. We'd need three trucks, plus Bessie. Six, we'd need six of the engineers, that's nearly the full adult team, leaving the apprentices in charge for what, a month? two?

I inch closer, apprehensive of the damage I'll find. I slide my hand up to the panel edge, warm steel, bolted and welded in place, nice and secure, and pull myself up to examine the glass.

That's when I see it, a miracle? Maybe, but definitely a game-changer.

I try to stay calm and buzz down to Malcolm, asking if he remembers that crazy story he told me about Hawaii, how they would wear a skirt made of grass, thick as your thumb and longer than your arm. He confirms, it's no story, he has pictures, why was I asking? I turn on my vid feed, ask him to record it, we'll need to keep the evidence.

Slowly, I hold up the impossible. A long thick blade of wild grass that has stuck to the dome.

BURNING AMBITION

BY JODIE HAMMOND

The Forest of Eden was a vast sea of greenery that went on for miles. A variety of different trees thrived within it and called this forest home. Tall pine trees stood proud amongst the smaller, more modest trees. Yet all their thick leaves united to create a collage of greens and ambers. Upon closer inspection, each pine tree was decorated with pinecones which were all a deep, woody brown colour. The sweet and earthy scent of the place was near overwhelming.

The sky was simply magnificent on this evening at the height of summer. If it had been sunset, some would surely have declared it the most picturesque sight Earth had ever seen. It was aglow with vibrant reds that faded into vivid, warm oranges, even the few trailing clouds reflecting the riot of colour. It was the sort of sight that every single person deserved to see at least once in their life, for Earth was simply beautiful; it was made to be enjoyed.

But such things had long been ignored. No one appreciated the simple pleasures that the Earth had to offer any longer.

Nor would they, until it was all gone.

*

Embers danced and swirled in the bloody sky as they gracefully drifted towards the ground, where they would perish and die out. Smoke rose from the burning peat. Once beautiful, green lawns were now scorched a bare terracotta.

Flower beds were now nothing more than a resting place for the withered remains of angelonias, chrysanthemums, and hydrangeas. They lay amongst broken and cracked pieces of clay plant pots.

The choking air smelt sickly sweet from the sap melting and weeping from the trees. And the char of pollen and petals added a distinctly unpleasant note and bitter flavour. Snaps, crackles and pops accompanied the flames that danced and ran between the tall tree trunks. The roar of fire drowned out all else as the wind whipped it up and urged it onwards.

Trees stood defenceless before the attack.

*

105 Bushway Lane was a modest build, with a wooden aesthetic. The house looked natural against the rigidly organised fir trees that lined the grounds like a security fence and isolated the house from the neighbouring houses, allowing the occupants to feel as though they lived in their own little world. The building was built with a bounty of different woods, including pine, spruce, oak, and cedar. It was an architectural triumph,

with nature as its trophy. It was a statement piece, declaring status, and to be envied.

Large windows reflected the ominous sky, staining the pure white interior of the house. Cinders and ash settled upon the furniture on the outdoor decking. Everything was becoming smeared and ruined.

Ben stood by the windows staring in pure horror. How could a place of such serenity have come to this? It was wrong, almost blasphemous! Their little peaceful corner of the world was under threat, and so were they.

Ben gazed at the menacing amber glow just beyond the tree line at the end of his garden.

The fire was spreading fast. Did they even have time?

What was mother nature doing to herself? How could the wind betray the trees like this?

*

The cries of a baby rose within the house. They echoed off every wall, making the new mother more anxious every second. Amelia was packing a bag with haste whilst her son screamed and wiggled on the bed. The fierce glow from the fire that blazed outside shone into the bedroom.

She had to hurry. They didn't have much time.

She was busy ramming clothes into a hiking backpack when Ben ran into the room and shoved bottles of water into it before handing Amelia the baby carrier. He helped her put it on before placing their son against her chest. The child calmed instantly as his forehead met the base of Amelia's neck. Skin on skin contact was what he needed.

'We have to get going, sweetheart. The fire isn't far off.' Ben lugged the bag onto his back before adjusting the straps against his shoulders. Amelia placed a muslin cloth over her son's head to prevent him from inhaling too much smoke.

The pair of new parents looked at each other for a second and nodded slightly. They silently promised each other that they would survive this, and they would ensure that their son was delivered to safety.

'Let's go.'

And with that, Amelia, Ben, and their son abandoned their perfect family home.

*

As soon as Ben and Amelia stepped out of the house, the acrid smoke of the burning forest caught in their throats and had them coughing. They hadn't anticipated how bad it would be. They looked up to the angry sky and realised just how high the flames must now be reaching.

Ash swirled around them, mocking the beautiful months of winter when flurries of snow would chase amongst the trees like sprites.

Would they ever see snow again? Amelia doubted it very much but tried to keep her mind focussed for her son.

Ben knew that they wouldn't be able to drive their way out as the fire had completely cut them off. The only option would be up the mountain, trying to keep ahead of the fire and above the thick smoke. As they started off through the trees, it was clear the ground cover wasn't faring well against the fire either. Most of the loose foliage was singed and, with every step, a sickening crunch sounded beneath their feet.

Amelia kept one hand firmly grasped in Ben's as they force-marched over fallen branches and uncovered roots, her other hand firmly on her son's head.

It wasn't just that she wanted to reassure him: she needed the reassurance herself that he was still there. Still with them.

They stopped for a short moment to catch their breaths and have a sip of water. Ben carefully pulled the muslin cloth off his son's head to see him peacefully sleeping and blissfully unaware of the dangers that surrounded their young family.

From this higher vantage point, he could already see whole areas where there was precious little of the forest left, save for the scattering of smoking trunks. In the distance, a Firewatch tower stood tall amid untouched reaches. It stood like a beacon of hope in the north.

They had to get there.

The roaring fires had spread to the east and west, split like the parting of the Red Sea. If they hurried, they should get to the Firewatch tower before the fires met up.

'Right, we're going to head for that Firewatch tower. There should be a ranger and a radio. It's our only chance.' Ben looked deeply into his wife's eyes. Even though she was dishevelled, sweaty and exhausted, she was still as beautiful as the day they'd sworn themselves to each other.

With a quick nod, Amelia took Ben's hand again as they forged on.

*

The dark had finally settled in the forest. Usually the night brought a calm, cool air which diminished the punishing humidity of the day. Yet tonight the temperature only rose higher and higher. Ben saw from his watch that they'd been on the move for three hours – surely they had to be close to safety now. Yet, more and more small fires were breaking out just behind them, and a couple ahead of them even.

Usually when one looked up this deep in the forest, the beams of the sun would refract through the foliage and send enchanting rainbows skipping across the moss, or the moon would pick out ghostly paths.

Not now. A black pall covered the sky.

As Ben and Amelia pressed onwards, phone-torches in hand, the ash particles were so thick that they all but formed an obscuring fog. Ben struggled to keep his bearings, praying he wasn't deluded in believing he might have some internal compass.

Their skin was gritty and smeared. They were overheated and exhausted from the pace they'd kept up. As Amelia passed a particularly large pine tree, she slowed and leaned against it, to take several laboured breaths under her make-shift mask. Ben stopped a metre ahead of her.

They were good people. They didn't deserve this hell. God had not abandoned them. He wouldn't. But Ben's faith and hope were threatening to desert him.

As he wiped the sweat from his brow, his torch caught something pale in the night. He should never have doubted. He pulled down his mask and grinned.

'Amelia, look!'

It was faint, but it was there. It was the base of the Firewatch tower. He moved over to his wife and son and placed a kiss on the baby's covered head.

'We're almost there, honey,' he murmured.

*

As the family reached the bottom of the Firewatch tower, they couldn't see any fire damage to it.

They were going to make it.

Perhaps their neighbours had made it here. If they'd all headed towards the tower, they could all get out together.

As Ben placed his hand on the steel railing, it near scalded his palm. Was the air becoming so superheated? They had to get inside the protection of the tower. Ben placed the mask from his face on the railing. He turned to his wife, who was affectionately stroking her son's back.

'Use the cloth. The railing's hot. I'm going to run up ahead and see if anyone's here.'

Ben went quickly up the stairs. Determination, hope, and a little fear drove his actions.

Amelia carefully followed him. At last, they were at a place where her son would be safe. And it was cooler, the higher she climbed.

Yet as she got to the top platform, she was dismayed. The fires spread as far as her eye could see. In every direction, there was a sea of orange and yellow flames. The dense black smoke blocked out the sky, and any sight of the heavens.

There were no paths through the fire anymore. They were surrounded.

Amelia turned and saw her husband in a state of panic. He was the only one in the tower. There was no ranger, and no other survivors. Were they the only ones left?

When Amelia entered the tower, she was shocked to see it turned upside down.

Papers and stationery were strewn over the ground, clothes and blankets thrown haphazardly on the makeshift camp bed. Cupboard doors were left hanging open, revealing everything had been taken.

Had there been a struggle?

Ben went and hunched over the table in front of a radio. He held the receiver in one hand and the other meddled with the dials.

'Hello?! Hello?! Does anybody copy? Hello?!'

All he received was static.

'No, no, no, NO!' Ben's shout made Amelia jump, startling their son, who started whimpering. Amelia started to rock and hum to him. As she stared back at her husband, she could see the glow from the fire colour his face.

It was getting closer.

'Please, if anyone copies, we are in Eden Forest. I'm not sure what tower. Please, I have my family here. Send help! I repeat, SOS!'

More static.

Ben threw the receiver down as he was racked by coughing. Amelia hurried to take a bottle of water from the bag and handed it to him. He swigged and went back to the radio, while Amelia grabbed a blanket from the bed and wedged it at the bottom of the door to prevent any smoke from getting in. She used some of the clothes to cover the windows as best she could.

Ben fiddled and fiddled with the dials, trying every station he could find, repeating the same message every time.

And getting the same answer.

Static.

Amelia saw the fierce flames getting higher, and the smoke getting thicker. And it was slowly getting inside.

'Ben...' Amelia whimpered.

'I'm trying, honey. I'm trying...' His voice quavered, betraying his fear.

As minutes passed, the tower began to heat up. Sweat soon rolled from their brows.

Ben still only received static.

They coughed more and more frequently, and made new masks for themselves. Even so, they struggled to breathe, while wiping their stinging eyes.

As they both sat on the floor beside the radio, Amelia rested the side of her leg against Ben's, seeking comfort. She rested her head against the wall behind her and tried to calm her son. His pitiful cries were heart-breaking. She felt numb, her body felt almost weightless.

Dedicated to the memories of Ben, Amelia, and Henry Walker

MOTHER'S CARE

BY GABRIELA HOUSTON

I push the tin over, revealing its ragged edge. If it held something appealing, once, maybe I would feel the moment's brief temptation to push my snout in, to brave the razor of the cut metal grazing my cheeks, and uncomfortably pressing on my whiskers. As it is, a cursory sniff reveals nothing that hasn't rotted into oblivion long ago.

A quiet falls over the house. It's outside of my territory and relaxing is out of the question. I have to go back soon anyway. My babies are hungry, and, more urgently still, exposed, in their warren. I have chased away the rabbit that had made it to shelter her own young. I was already heavy and knew my babies would come soon. The rabbit put up a decent fight of course, as her kind do, with their brutal kicks, and the boxing of the most delicate parts of the nose. I got the best of her though, as she knew I would. I could hear her sorrow as I slithered into her home. Her children were still small and blind. Exposed and helpless.

As mine are now, and the irony is not lost on me.

The Last Horizon

An irregular sound carries across the dust-covered floor. Something scampers away as the wind bats at the broken door. The door itself holds onto its rusted hinges by nothing more than a thread of metal and memory. And perhaps also the weeds and the ivy crawling across the floor, the tendrils grabbing thirstily onto the crumbling plaster of the walls.

A movement and within a heartbeat I catch the mouse. It wriggles in my mouth, making small, scared noises. I shake my head once, twice and its body hangs limp in my mouth. I press my jaws together, and the metallic taste hits my palate. An appetiser, but I can't stay here to eat. Already I can hear the howling of the dog pack running down the street. I can't be here when they arrive.

I climb up the collapsed shed adjoining the house then onto a tree branch and up to the roof. I can enjoy my meal here, as well as observe the world around. The dogs are nearing, running close together, like an arrow with the leader at the front. A huge grey dog, still keeping most of its working forebears' shape, with the mane and the ridiculously low behind. The shapes of his followers are all a mix, some large and cumbersome, some lean, some small and yappy. All of them hungry though, and so I keep to my hiding place.

I can't understand this need of theirs, to join into a herd in such a way. To pick a leader, somebody to follow. Perhaps, though generations have passed, they still feel that longing for their masters, telling them what and when to eat, when to run, even when to piss.

Cats are made of sterner stuff, of course. We remember, but romanticise nothing. We remember it all, exactly as it was. And we don't miss those who would have ruled over us.

I lick my paw, stained with the mouse intestines. Their juices dribble between my toes and I stretch them out to allow my tongue to pass freely in the gap.

One of the dogs lifts its snout up, sniffing the air. I flatten myself against the roof. Did it catch the scent of my meal? Of me? But no, they howl and turn towards the meadow between the collapsed buildings. A hint of red. I blink once, slowly, as the sun warms my bones. The fox will not outrun them, but with a little bit of luck will take them far enough so I won't need to worry for a while. I whisper no prayer to the winds on the fox's behalf. It wouldn't return the favour.

Satisfied there are no more predators nearby, I climb down. A crumbling tile falls off the roof, clattering down. The lush foliage muffles the sound, but there are many ears as keen as mine. I freeze for a moment, and scamper away.

I trot between the shrubs overtaking the cracked surface of the road, still visible between the weeds, still heating into dark pools when the sun is up, burning the pads of your paws if you don't watch where you're going.

A magpie screeches at me from her perch on a tall grey pillar, its top a jagged mess of broken glass, the angry maws to deter any land dwellers.

I follow the path back to the warren slowly, cautiously. Confuse the trail, confuse the scent. I reach the familiar opening, but something's not right.

I stand in the shadow, frozen to the ground. An old hound, its sides scarred and sunken. An old male, too slow and sick to be a part of the pack anymore, searching for the easier prey. He sniffs the air, and throws himself to the opening of my warren, scratching and digging at the soil, the muzzle forced into the ground.

The fur on my neck stands up and a hiss escapes my lungs. The hound turns towards me with a growl. His left eye is white. I take note of the fact while I circle around on stiff legs, trying to make myself large. I'm not fooling anyone. I'm big for my kind, but a hound could tear the neck of a deer if supported by the pack. Yet my claws are sharp and my teeth can do real damage. I can see the hound assessing me and turning back to the warren, where my babies sleep dreaming of warm milk.

I lunge at the trespasser. I bounce off his back, avoid his teeth and pounce back. Claws out, I target his head, trying to scratch at his good eye. Got his attention now. He growls, a deep guttural sound.

He turns away from the warren and walks towards me, slowly. Blood drips from his muzzle where my claws made contact. But not enough, not nearly enough. One bite of those huge jaws and he'll break me in half. We both know it, and I can see the quiet satisfaction in his one good eye. He's sure of the kill, and if I don't judge the moment right, I will only prove him right.

I sense the moment he's about to jump. The tensing of his shoulders, the lowering of his behind, all my spies telling me to duck. And I do, the hound's jaws snapping shut where I stood a moment before.

I could climb up the tree, of course I could. He'd bark up at me for a moment, and then turn back to the warren. I need a different tactic.

I run ahead, leading him through the thick undergrowth, the dew drops wetting my fur as I dash between the bushes. I feel the air move and I jump to the side, as his jaws search for my flesh. I try to keep on the dog's blind side, as he snaps at me again and again. I lead him through the brambles, the long thorns tearing at the skin of my ears. Their brutal combing will slow the hound down though, and limit his movements so that I can jump at his neck and tear a piece of fur right above his right eye, before bouncing off again.

The dog is tiring now. I must not let him get too tired to chase. Not so tired he might remember the smell of my babies in their home.

The hound howls, the ghastly noise rending the air. He was strong once. Maybe a leader of the pack even. The age hasn't humbled him enough to keep him quiet. He's panting. His flank moves in short rugged bursts, like he can't quite bring enough air into his lungs. He stands straight and looks back.

No.

Not a chance.

I bounce of him again, bite the ear. A piece of it tears, leaving a taste of blood in my mouth. The hound shakes me off, and throws me against the tree, growing out of the corroded remains of some large metal box. I'm dazed for a moment only. A moment too long. The dog is getting closer, wary, but sure of me now.

A growl sounds in the air. I blink my confusion away. The hound looks up, alarmed. As he should be.

The dogs enter the clearing: hungry and vicious bandits, the smell of the fox they'd caught still drying on their fur. None of them notice as I climb up the tree, though whatever of my smell lingers is still enough to raise the hackles on some of them.

The pack surrounds the hound. It cowers, invokes the bonds of brotherhood with a whine. I watch while the pack kills the hound. Quickly, efficiently. They feast and they leave.

When they're well and truly gone I trot back to the warren. I slither in, the smell of my children is soothing. I'd been gone longer than usual and they're hungry.

I lie down next to them and nudge their small wriggling bodies towards me so they can feed.

When they finish I will bathe them with my tongue, tickling their soft bellies. Then I will sleep, surrounded by their warmth. Relaxing in the moment of safety hard won.

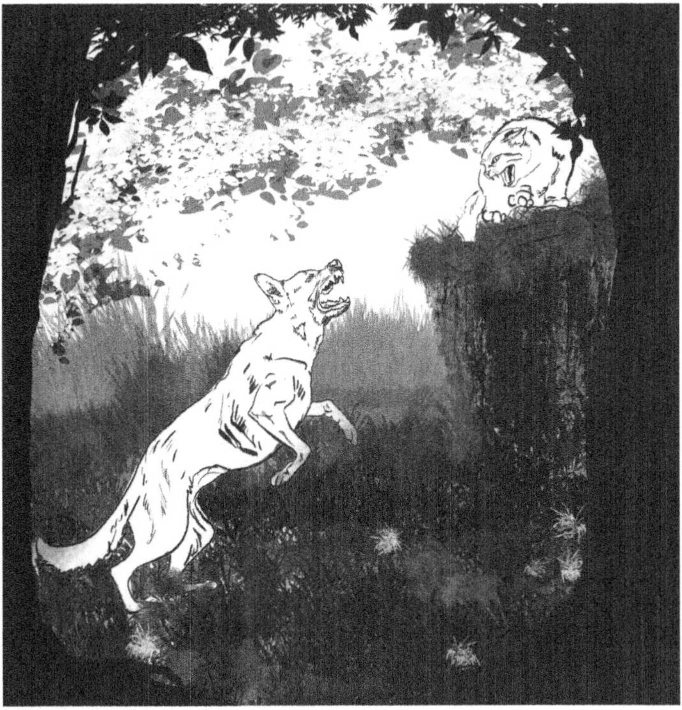

UNICORN RISING

BY A J DALTON

What the hell am I doing? I must be insane. My lungs and thighs were burning. *I haven't had this much exercise in decades.* The sky was the colour of the Scottish flag. *Of course it is, idiot.* The air was exhausting, it was so clean. *It's probably putting years on your life expectancy... as long as you survive this!* Its rush filled my ears, almost ridding me of the tinnitus I'd developed from a lifetime of living in London.

I dropped down onto the grass, looking to catch my rasping breath. The granite beneath the sod refused to yield even a fraction. *Maybe you should head back to your lodgings and try again tomorrow. No, your muscles will be so sore you might never leave your bed again. And that sour-faced landlady will heap even more dour and silent disapproval upon you, for being a soft southerner who should never have ventured to these far-flung crags in the first place. Maybe you should have explained you'd come to see if there really were unicorns living on the most remote mountain in Scotland.*

No, that's right, you couldn't do that, because she'd rightly surmise you were as mad as a brush.

The Last Horizon

*

Maria had given me the sort of out-of-place frown of which only the innocent faces of children were capable. 'Don't be silly, daddy. Everyone *knows* the unicorns were wiped out in old Greece and they had to run away to distant places like the Highlands of Scotland. That's why unicorns are the symbol of that place, *silly*!'

My wife had nodded conspicuously while she'd made our toast that morning. 'Susan,' I'd murmured from the corner of my mouth, 'you really aren't helping. Look, sweet daughter o' mine, why don't people ever report seeing these unicorns, then?'

She looked at me incredulously, as if I was literally the dumbest man on the planet (a look she'd surely learnt from Susan… or not). 'Da-a-addy, the unicorns are invisible. They have to be that way to stop people hunting them for their horns. It's soooo obvious!' ("Obvious" was her latest word. Sheesh.)

'Ohh, they're invisible,' I realised. 'Like the invisible friend you had when you were five?'

Her scorn couldn't have been greater. 'Just because you couldn't see Jessica doesn't mean she wasn't there. *You* made her leave cos you're so *mean*!'

Susan shot me a warning glance and I raised my hands. 'Alright, alright. I've already apologised about that. Back to the unicorns, then.' I smiled. 'If there are all these unicorns in the Highlands, is the place covered in unicorn pooh? Big mounds of it? Or is it invisible pooh?'

'Roy!' Susan had laughed in protest.

Maria had cracked and giggled, clapping in the delighted way that she had. 'It is…' She snorted like a horse, making her laugh more. 'It is manure for the grass, daddy!'

'Are the mountains made of unicorn pooh? The pooh mountains aren't invisible, then. Are the Highlands only there because of thousands of years of poohing unicorns?'

She'd cried with joy, till her sides had hurt. 'Stop it, stop it! Owww!'

'Tell you what, sweetheart, I'll go check these mountains for you, but I imagine we could smell them from London if there really was that much pooh, invisible or not!'

*

And work had told me to take time off, because orders were down for the time of year, although we were due a bigger order from a regular client in a few weeks. Aaaanyway, I was suddenly stuck at home, at a bit of a loss, while Susan was out at work everyday and Maria was off to school.

'You promised to go find the unicorns, daddy. You *promised*!' Maria had said pointedly one evening when I complained about not having done much except sleep, play a computer game or two, and watch an utterly dreadful and dubbed Netflix movie about dragons.

I glanced at Susan, who raised her eyebrows and shoulders in one. 'You *did* promise, Roy,' she said all innocently. 'Come on, why don't you get away for a few days, rather than moping around here?'

'Eh? Are you trying to get rid of me or something?'

'Of course I am, sweetheart.' Maria giggled and nodded at that. They loved to gang up on me, but I liked it like that somehow.

'Well, that's charming. The Highlands are too far. Time and money.'

'Not if you get a budget flight from Heathrow and then

a local train. What's the name of that whisky distillery you've always talked about wanting to visit, hmm?'

'Wolfburn, in Thurso,' I groused. 'It's the most northern of the highland distilleries.'

'Don't you have ancestors from around that way or something?'

'You know full well I do, Susan.'

'So? Well?'

I looked at the two girls I loved most in the world and sighed. How could I say no? Besides, it might be good for me, and I *had* promised. I hadn't yet broken a promise to Maria, and I wasn't about to start then.

*

But I was flaming regretting it now, I can tell you. The distillery had been closed when I'd arrived, because the owner was on a business trip or something ludicrous. None of the monosyllabic locals had ever heard of my ancestors – my tersely funereal landlady was positively chatty by comparison. And it wouldn't stop goddamn drizzling! With its exposed and northerly location, Thurso had to be one of the most grimly Scottish places in Scotland.

All that said, maybe they were actually in mourning. After all, just the week before, the popular Scottish PM had suddenly collapsed clutching her chest during an impassioned speech (was there any other type?) in Parliament about needing to expand mining activity and industry into the Highlands. Maria, who'd watched it happen on live TV, I'm distressed to say, had been fairly unfazed, nodding and explaining that an invisible unicorn had plunged its horn through the PM's chest, to prevent any further invasion of their last refuge and habitat.

'I don't think unicorns follow current affairs, sweetie,' I'd replied dubiously.

'Adults and people don't just suddenly die, daddy!' Maria had yelled, heat, panic and anger all mixed.

Susan had suddenly been there, putting her arm around Maria's shaking shoulders, shushing her, reassuring her. My wife had given me such a look – upbraiding, pleading, demanding – that I found myself mimicking her slow nod and saying, 'Y-yes! I was confused, sweetie. Daddy now understands it was a unicorn. Sorry. Say you forgive me. Breathe. It's all fine. Just breathe, sweetie. She was taken by the invisible unicorn.'

*

'What am I doing?' I gasped, struggling to breathe, like I was hyperventilating. I was barely halfway up the crag – it was gonna be the death of me. I distractedly wondered if it was fairly painless being dead, and if living and breathing, rather, was the excruciatingly painful and tragic state to be in. It certainly felt that way. 'Sh-sh-should never have given up that gym membership, you idiot, Roy. Christ!'

I looked up ahead of me. It was so far... maybe too far? I checked my phone. Of course, there was no signal. No mountain rescue, then. Besides, that would be a wus's way out. I'd end up in all the local papers, and the Scots would have a chuckle at the dumb lowlander's expense – still, it might at least cheer them up a bit.

I don't how long I lay there in the drizzle – long enough to start shivering though. Oddly there was no one else crazy enough to be out and about, so there was no obvious helping hand in prospect. I had to get moving or exposure and hypothermia would be the ones who found me.

I slowly ratcheted myself up and got my feet under me. 'Get moving, Roy. That's the best way to warm up! Come on. What would your ancestors say if they saw you like this? You'd be a disgrace to the entire family line.'

I desperately wanted to go back down to the shelter of Thurso, but I knew I'd never attempt the climb again. I'd have wasted the trip. I'd have failed. And I'd have to return home with my tail between my legs. I wouldn't be able to look either Susan or Maria in the eyes as I admitted I'd failed... or lie that I'd made it up the crag. And if I lied, what would I say I'd found? Nothing? Unicorns which I couldn't see... which was the same as nothing? But my girls would know I was lying. And I'd never lied to them before. Something would be *broken*, whether it was their faith in my ability when I confessed to failure, or whether it was their trust when they heard me lie. I'd be broken, and I'd break our close family. How could I do that? I'd *promised* my dear Maria. I wouldn't break that promise. I'd rather die as an ill-prepared idiot on these slops than do that to her.

I peered up towards the heights of the crag, which loomed darkly against the grey foment of the heavens, a grey that darkened towards a deathly black on the crag beyond that. Wiping a trembling hand across my brow, I pushed on, careful of each slippery step on the sward, measuring each breath like a geriatric. I felt my age. And I felt my insignificance against the enduring Highlands, too.

No wonder there were those who were threatened – or made to feel inadequate – by such unyielding majesty. No wonder they conspired, toiled and strove to build vast machines that might trammel the earth and rock, hoping one day to pummel the entire landscape, if not the world, into obedience and ultimately their own broken image. What vanity was it in us – when realising our own comparative ugliness – to seek to damage, mar and scar that which was more than ourselves. We were selfish and self-indulged children, perhaps. Even so, I bent, straightened, levered and pulleyed myself upwards, an engine hellbent on conquering rather than being conquered.

It was ego that saw me keep going, I'm not too proud to admit. That and the knowledge that capitulation would probably have been the end of me anyway. And so it was, with a hoarse yell of defiance and triumph, that I forged my way over the top of that black crag!

Triumph, did I say? You should rightly be laughing about now. For what did I win myself in my folly? What hallowed place of self-realisation did I attain? Why, I stepped into the middle of the very storm, of course. Winds picked me up, hurling me hither and thither. They dangled me far out over the edge and I was sure I would be dashed down at the base of nature's edifice, or sent spinning back as far as Thurso itself. Lightning cackled, crackled and danced around me, mocking my impotence, former arrogance and disorientation. Dark creatures of chaos cavorted, taunted and tormented. All swirled and spun.

'Mercy!' I shrieked to the heavens, huddling to try and protect myself, in my fear and shame. I squeezed my eyes shut in prayer.

And in that moment, there was stillness. I dared look around me then, or so I thought, in a confused wonder or dream. Was this the eye of the storm? The weather rampaged silently across the other crags but, here, a shaft of sunlight speared down upon the summit. Rain sheeted down, rainbows arcing all around, creating dazzling bridges and after-images. And that rain stopped many hands short of the ground, outlining a wide herd of horses. The largest among them reared, then, the sun sparkling from the very tip of its horn. There, upon its back, although perhaps I imagined it, was a small figure pointing me on to the farthest, highest and darkest of the crags, but I knew that to be a place for the dead, so I dared not proceed one step further.

*

How I rushed home, to London. I burst through the front door, immediately calling for Maria.

Susan was there. 'Oh, thank God!' she cried, clasping me to her. 'I've been worried sick. Where have you *been*?'

'Where's Maria? I need to tell her.'

She gently took me by the hand. 'Come through to the kitchen. I'll put the kettle on.'

'The unicorns are real, Susan!'

'Look at the state of you, sweetheart. Have you been sleeping outside?'

'I went to Thurso, didn't I tell you? To find the unicorns.'

'Here you go. Cuppa tea. Take a sip… That's good.'

'Is Maria at school? What day is it?'

She gave me the sort of smile that… well, Cleopatra might have given to Enobarbus, or Mark Anthony… and then as she would give to her most beloved Roy McNairn. 'Okay, sweetie, take my hands. Let's remember together, shall we? Maria died, yes?'

'When? What are you talking about?'

'The Scottish PM–'

'Died giving the speech.'

'No, sweetheart. Maria died because of her weak heart, remember? But you blamed the PM, who was making some speech on the TV. You got things confused, sweetheart. We spoke with the grief counsellor about this, didn't we?'

I waited. 'Yes. And I saw her, Susan. I saw Maria with the

unicorns. They're real, and living up there in the Highlands! That's where I went, you see, just like I promised her. It was beautiful. And Maria was there. You do believe me, don't you?'

She smiled. 'Of course I do, sweetheart.'

'Because she's safe now. It's going to be okay, Susan... isn't it?'

She rested her hands on mine and gazed kindly into my eyes. 'Yes, sweetheart, it's going to be okay.'

LITTLE FISH, BIG POND

BY MATT RYDER

Dephelle gazed out across the golden beach, crystalline turquoise waters casually nipping at the shore. Her three children were playing together spiritedly, if a little boisterously, alternating between construction of a child-sized sand fortress and dips in the refreshing waters whenever the intense heat became a little too much. Phoe was shrieking excitedly and running away from her brothers as they chased her down, determined to give her a damn good soaking with their overpriced waterguns – a recent gift from their ever-doting grandmother.

Sighing contentedly, she lay back once more and relaxed into the fine grains of sand. Life was getting to be too much fun.

'Dephi baby, time to go! Kids! Come on!' came the call from behind her. She half-turned and smiled as her eyes met her husband's, who was beckoning to them all somewhat impatiently. She rose languidly, clasped her hands behind her head and stretched into the glowing warmth of the sun.

'Kids! Now!' The call was repeated with a greater sense of urgency. Dephelle lazily meandered up to her husband and wrapped her arms around him.

'What's the rush honey? Look, they're having a great time.' She smiled and nodded towards their children. 'And we've got nothing on today. Come down to the beach and relax.'

'Work just called, they need me to go in. Sorry baby.'

Dephelle's eyes narrowed. 'It's not your rota today. Say no!'

'I can't, it's important. Sorry baby.'

'Fine. I'm staying here with the kids for a bit.' She pulled away impetuously and started back for the beach. 'What time will you be home?'

'Don't know yet.'

Dephelle pouted her lips in displeasure. 'Whatever Karulan.'

He knew he'd upset her – she only ever used his name when she was particularly annoyed. Sighing, he yelled 'Bye kids!' and gave a big wave, which was nonchalantly returned before the three children resumed their play. Karulan's thoughts drifted onto work. Sighing once more, he headed in.

*

'I can't figure out what the drokk is happening here.'

Celikidha stared at the array of screens displaying various sets of global data and statistics: wind currents, seismic activity, UV levels, tidal data and atmospheric content were currently visible overlaying a large global map. She had been stationed on the satellite observation post Dekro Laviid studying the bipeds – they referred to themselves as *human* – for over five thousand planetary day/night cycles. Her expertise combined with the station's banks of sensor arrays could predict events on the planet with far greater accuracy than the natives' own forecasts. Or at least that was the case up until two standard Earth years ago.

'Take a break Celik. You haven't shifted from that chair for so long I'm beginning to think you're fused to it.' Chief Scientist Ulondru spoke with a deep rumble, the kindness apparent in his voice. He was probably right; she should go work off some of this tension.

'Yeah, alright. Let me just set up a couple more sims and I'll hit the gym for a bit.'

She configured the simulation parameters to her liking via her neural implant, invoking a wall of screens on her left to burst into life; ever-changing torrents of patterns and data were brilliantly displayed. She rose and headed to the room's sole doorway, making a final appraisal of the data as she walked by the freshly operational screen bank and giving Ulondru a casual wave as she exited.

'Later Chief.'

Gravity on the station was set to match that of her homeworld some few hundred light years distant; approximately nine tenths that of the observed planet. Celikidha travelled through the brightly lit corridors to the gymnasium and, before starting her workout, unconsciously increased the room's gravity to Earth standard. She snapped back to the present, wondering what had prompted her to make the adjustment. Was she actually planning on visiting the planet? No, that was forbidden – policy dictated that Dekro Laviid was solely passive with its observations and would take no part in influencing events, regardless of how cataclysmic they may be. She reflected that it wasn't so long ago that predictions for the humans bringing about their own nuclear apocalypse had reached a likelihood of 81%, and even then station policy had held firm. Thankfully tensions had since eased - that was a particular fireworks display none of the crew wished to see.

She hopped onto the treadmill and relayed a command, setting it to a comfortable warm-up speed, then settled into a groove, the rhythmic thumping of her feet reassuring. A second command was sent to the generous monitor attached to the opposite wall, which responded by displaying miniature live feeds of several human broadcasts in grid formation. Celikidha had come to not just appreciate, but actively enjoy these alien transmissions and allowed herself this small indulgence, bizarre as it seemed to her crewmates. She enlarged a program depicting the human's favourite sport, and watched the players run around chasing a ball for a few seconds before flicking to another; like many of the transmissions this next one was a report on their current global crisis. Increasing the display's volume, she focused her attention on the screen which displayed a human standing before a wide trench.

'As you can see behind me,' the human was saying, one of their more famous landmarks (St. Pauls Cathedral Celikidha recalled) in camera shot, 'people are actually able to cross The River Thames during low tide.' The camera panned slightly to the left to show the miniscule amount of water barely covering the riverbed with many humans traversing the trench, meandering around the larger puddles.

Celikidha snorted and flicked to the next program. A wizened human was speaking slowly, their voice trembling with apparent age:

'…the events of these past two decades; the unprecedented Eastern alliance between Russia and China. So much global tension with Russia attempting to recreate the Soviet Union of the 1960s. Their eagerness to extend their border to Europe was backed not only by a finger over the red button, but they also had China's economic powerhouse on their side.' The human paused for a moment, overcome with emotion.

'Of course, we, along with other Western nations, introduced a multitude of sanctions, but the Russians responded by retreating into economic isolation. They persuaded China to restrict exports of the mass-produced technology we in the West had become so hungry for and reliant upon. Gas supplies that fed directly to Germany were cut, arable yields never passed the new 'Iron Curtain', and there were plenty of Eastern nations demanding crude oil. It was like the world split in two.' The human paused once again, eyes moist.

'The upside to this for us was a flurry of manufacturing. We created power plants that did not rely upon gas. We had clean, self-sufficient energy, more than enough to accommodate the massive production run of electric vehicles. Many countries' governments offered grants for the installation of solar panels to a great many homes and businesses. At long last Mother Earth was being respected.'

'And yet, something went wrong.'

Tears were gently rolling down the human's face as they spoke this final line. Unable to bear the grief seemingly pervading the gym, Celikidha switched the program once again, the next one discussing failed wind farms. On-screen were hundreds of acres of offshore wind turbines, now mostly collapsed due to the drastic fall in sea level removing the buoyancy essential for their floating foundations. She had watched many similar programs; it was likely she had previously seen this exact transmission as the humans loved to repeat the same content over and over. Disinterested, she steeled her emotions and returned to the aged human's recollections, who was still speaking with a tremulous voice:

'The world's best minds simply have no explanation. The entire globe is in a state of panic; for the first time in two decades, the East and West are fighting a common enemy. Life itself.'

Celikidha powered down the screen, consumed by the

The Last Horizon

constant inexplicable problem that had fortuitously helped bring the warlike nations of Earth together in solidarity:

Where was the water?

Science, ever comforting, had become her opponent. On this world, one plus one equalled three. Celikidha had absorbed the human estimations of the planet's five Ice Age periods across the millennia and naturally ran her own simulations (there had actually been six), concluding that the next one was due to begin some one-to-five thousand years hence. The human's recent global efforts – or the majority at least – to combat what they labelled 'climate change' were paying off. Celikidha agreed with the human from the program; they were at last starting to do all the right things. Sea level typically only fell during a hydrologic cycle, but the ice sheets had remained relatively stable for centuries.

The fact that the current level was twenty metres lower than just a few short years ago was an enigma.

'Drokk it.' This was meant to be cleansing time, a chance to purge herself of the all-encompassing problem nagging incessantly at her psyche. She increased the treadmill's speed, again and again, pushing herself hard. Soon enough it was all she could do to control her breath, her rhythm; focusing fully on the physical as her hearts pounded in her chest and her fur became matted with sweat. She was deeply in the zone. Celikidha's internal timer surprised her when it expired to signify the end of her session, the notification gently flashing at the top leftmost area of her vision.

She hit the shower, body aching with the familiar glow of exertion. As the near-scolding jets of water soothed her agitated muscles, her mind unconsciously wrestled with the problem once more. Every scan had been repeated multiple times, every piece of data was accurate.

'This defies *everything*!' She spat the words fiercely, then, noticing her fists were tightly clenched, took a deep breath and forced herself to relax.

She adjusted the shower, switching the palliative heat to awakening chill, forcing herself to endure the sudden shift in temperature while admiring the thick, luxurious brown fur coating her pale blue skin as it prickled with goosebumps. Refreshed, she terminated the shower and activated the airstream, the warm jets flowing through her fur. She stepped out after a short time, accepting the slight dampness that still lingered. *Damp will have to do.* Dressing hurriedly, eager to see the results of her latest simulations, she headed back to the laboratory.

*

Kerulan was swimming lengths of the pool adjacent to his workplace, his powerful muscles propelling him through the water with ease. He had arrived shortly after receiving the urgent call to discover that the issue at the plant, whatever it was, required assessment by another specialist team before he was allowed to gain entry.

Typical. I abandoned a day out with my family for this and they aren't even ready for me.

Kerulan was naturally impatient, and the pool had beckoned eagerly. An easy decision. He'd completed several lengths when a shout came from the poolside: 'Kerulan! You're up.'

Recognising the voice as that of his supervisor, he halted his strokes. Treading water he replied, 'About time. Can you tell me what's going on now?'

'Get dressed and meet me inside. We'll talk there.' His supervisor turned and headed for the plant.

All thoughts of the beach quickly evaporating, Kerulan nimbly climbed out and headed for the changing rooms.

The Last Horizon

✻

Entering briskly, Celikidha strode to the bank of screens. Regarding them in quiet contemplation, she remained motionless but for her eyes flicking from one display to another as if absorbing a surrealist exhibit, fastidiously trying to delve into the mind of the artist. Her eyes narrowed momentarily as she sent a command to the array, exchanging one dataset for another on a couple of the displays.

There.

'Chief, come see this.' She spoke without turning her head as she continued to stare at a row of adjacent screens.

'What have you got?' Ulondru stepped towards her quizzically, following her gaze.

'Look at this row. Historical oceanic currents data: years three, two and one. Compare them to this screen.'

She gestured at a neighbouring display. 'This is *now*. Do you see it?' Celikidha froze the screens on a view of the South Pacific; a chain of oceanic eddies somewhat south of New Zealand meandered to The Cape of Good Hope on the southern tip of Africa.

Ulondru took a pace forward, joining Celikidha in motionless appraisal.

'I see it. This current has developed a slight northward trend. Subtle, but yes.' He pointed at the part of the Antarctic Circumpolar Current surrounding the north shore of the continent.

'What do you think?' Celikidha asked, certain that she wouldn't receive a meaningful answer. After so many years of meticulous study she knew the harmony of this planet better than anyone, even the Chief Scientist.

Ulondru turned met her gaze with a slight smile on his face.

'I don't know, but you *knew* I'd say that, right?'

'Can we send—'

Ulondru cut her off with a sharp wave of his hand and paused. Drawing a sharp intake of breath before exhaling through his nostrils, he was deep in contemplation and seemingly lost for a moment in his thoughts. The potential fallout of any such decision – which was completely without precedent – rested on solely him as the station's Chief of Staff, and thus far he had carefully cultivated their species' ethos of passive observation.

Decision made, Ulondru regarded Celikidha once more. 'Yes, we can send a drone.' He said the words playfully, his smile enlarging to display a large mouth filled with pointed teeth.

'Yes! At last!' Celikidha punched the air victoriously; she had been stating her case to send a scout drone to Earth ever since she'd arrived. It was all well and good utilising the station's comprehensive array of sensors, as well as connecting to the humans' data network – their complete archives were stored within the station for analysis, and she considered herself an expert on human history – but she had been aching to get a little more... personal.

Without hesitation she dropped into her chair and began sending commands to the station to prepare one of its drones for launch. Screens altered their displays to relay relevant information, 3D models of the drone were depicted on a number of them.

If the humans saw this, they'd think it was a tiny replica of London's Gherkin.

She smiled at this unbidden thought. Not that they would of course; the technology incorporated into the drone was far beyond the human's current capabilities. Given time they may even reach the required level of technological advancement themselves, assuming they managed to meaningfully explore space beyond their solar system before either nuking themselves into oblivion or draining their "Mother" Earth of its resources. Her smile dropped at this darker thought; she was invested in this planet and its people and couldn't – or wouldn't – understand why intervention was prohibited. If only she could show the bipeds the possibilities of what they could achieve, how much more existed beyond their tiny globe orbiting just one out of billions of stars in this galaxy alone. It wouldn't need much more than a quick demonstration of–

'Everything okay?' Ulondru's voice brought her back to reality in a flash.

'Finalising now Chief,' she replied as she confirmed the parameters. 'Configuration verified. Ready to launch.'

'Send it.'

Celikidha felt an unbridled rush of excitement as she initiated the launch command, a faint pulse of vibration reverberating throughout the station as the drone exited the launch chamber at high velocity.

'Drone deployed. ETA eleven minutes fifty-five seconds.'

They monitored the drone's readouts during the spaceflight, aware that this was a historical moment for both themselves and the station; this mission was the first (and very possibly the last) close contact between the races.

*

'What the drokk just happened!?'

Celikidha pulled up all the last-known data regarding the drone, furiously demanding answers from the displays. The deployment had been textbook: optimal speed, atmospheric entry point and descent; all readings well within limits. Marine entry had been equally exemplary, the drone hitting the ocean at the designated spot of the north Antarctic Circumpolar Current before quickly submerging to seabed depth and heading further north.

Then the drone inexplicably disappeared.

Ulondru silently stepped back to the second screen bank and initiated his own diagnostics. The pair worked feverishly, independently, and yet in tandem, interrogating the final sensory data for a clue, some tiny irregularity that could lead to an explanation of the drone's sudden demise.

'Anything?' His tone was calm and composed; a complete contradiction to Celikidha's antagonised turmoil of emotion.

'Nothing yet Chief,' she replied, her voice urgent.

They continued their investigation in near silence for some considerable time, one or the other piping up occasionally with a potential lead, each instance ultimately proving false.

Eventually Ulondru spoke, 'We've done enough for now. I need to go and report this, plus we should both get some rest. Let's reconvene in eight hours.'

Celikidha looked at him mutely. He gave a tired smile in return before speaking gently, 'This has certainly been a day to remember – we've both launched and lost the first drone since this station was constructed. Who knows, maybe we'll be able to launch a second drone to find the first?'

'Yeah? We'll be out of drones in eight days at that rate,' she replied grumpily.

'Let's see what command come back with. But for now, rest. I'll recalibrate the communication scanners to listen out for any human chatter related to our drone while we recuperate. Let's go.'

She rose from the chair with a sigh and followed the chief out the door. They stopped outside their cabins, one opposite the other.

'Night Chief.'

'Night Celik.'

Sleep did not come easily, and when she awoke it felt as if she had only just closed her eyes. She activated her neural implants, the miniscule time display at the upper left of her vision informing her that she had almost an hour.

Forty-five minutes later, showered and breakfasted, she entered the lab. Chief Scientist Ulondru was already present, speaking with two other crewmates who turned and gave a wave as Celikidha approached. They were also scientists, both competent but lacking Celikidha's experience – and if she was being honest with herself, also lacking her own finely-honed instincts. She sat down next to them and tuned into Ulondru's briefing, which quickly brought her up to date with the current situation. Command had replied; their stance was that because observation post Dekro Laviid had the most complete data regarding the drone's disappearance, total decision-making autonomy in terms of how to proceed had been granted.

Ulondru continued, 'So Celik, I've assigned Kykilri and Colag to the lab to monitor in your stead. You'll be piloting the craft down to Earth for reconnaissance.'

Celikidha blinked, stunned. She'd never dared hope that the chance would come to visit this alien world, the backdrop to her life on Dekro Laviid. She was barely able to control her instinct to whoop with joy, but a certain decorum had to be maintained in front of the juniors.

'Yes SIR!' she boomed. 'Now?'

'Affirmative. Go suit up then head to the launch bay while we prep the craft. We'll complete final briefing during descent.'

'On it Chief,' and with that she stood and headed briskly to the exit, her excitement increasing palpably with every step.

*

The craft entered the ocean with the grace of a gannet diving and darting for shoals, some forty-five hyats north of the preceding drone's last known position. Celik mused that the distance was approximately fifteen miles in human measurements.

Damn, I'm even starting to think like them.

She sent the command to descend the nine hyats to the sea floor; the ship responded instantly, the sleek hull arching smoothly downwards. Her neural implants were linked to the ship's comprehensive AI controlling the vessel, which was far more capable of reacting to sensory data or perceived threats than any biological life form – nanoseconds rather than milliseconds.

As the craft neared the target depth, Celikidha yet again interrogated its military systems: a raft of pure energy cannons and magnetic coilguns, projectional stabiliser shields and decoy drones, all in addition to the ship's AI-powered camouflage which blended perfectly with their surroundings, no matter how bland or complex. The craft was effectively impervious to primitive human engineering. Celikidha was no soldier but was nonetheless comforted by the reassuring hum of the powerful vessel.

The ship levelled off and pointed its bow at the target destination. Celikdha's excitement grew with each passing hyat as she observed the passing marine life via the vessel's plethora of multi-spectrum cameras. Everything looked so... alien. With tentacles – so many tentacles. She continued to gaze in wonderment shadowed by a touch of fear. What if it wasn't the humans who destroyed the drone, but some giant sea monster? Humans never grew tired of speculating about ancient sea-faring behemoths, regardless of the apparent lack of proof. She shuddered inwardly and checked the readout.

She spoke into her helmet: 'Just over three hyats to the destination point Chief.'

'We see you. Watch your step out there.'

'Understood.'

As the craft edged closer, the tension was clearly palpable over the helmet mic, everyone in the station control room fully focused on the steady streams of received data. Celikidha, feeling foolish, chuckled inwardly; there was no way a giant sea monster could sneak up on—

The craft lurched violently as a smattering of insistent red alarms crowded her vision, her stomach lurching in equal measure.

'Celik!' came the cry from the helmet speaker.

She appraised the situation as the ship completed its rotation to come fully one hundred and eighty degrees. Something had *grabbed* the vessel, and the AI had responded instantly, deploying projectional shields while simultaneously performing a hard U-turn, aiming for an escape vector – she felt the engines power up for immediate exit. The craft increased its velocity.

Backwards.

'Celik! Talk to me!' repeated the cry in her ear.

The AI fired a barrage of munitions and searing energy beams in scatter formation, aiming at some unseen enemy. Celik checked the sensor data: zero threats identified. The gunfire fizzled into the distance, passing through and obliterating a number of aquatic animals enroute.

Still accelerating backward, the AI delivered more power to the engines while alternately banking from port to starboard in a bid to break free. The effort was futile; whatever held its subterranean grasp upon the ship was irresistible.

She glanced at the monitors – nothing but the blue of the ocean – then yelled into the mic: 'Something's got us Chief!' She saw that the engines were now at full throttle and yet they were still going the wrong way – backwards towards the seabed.

A fresh notification flashed up in her vision; something had been detected two hyats away. Whatever it was, she was on a collision course straight for it.

'Get out of therzzztt…' Ulondru's order distorted in her ear. She attempted to hail him over and over as she descended at a terrifyingly ever-quickening pace, but to no avail.

The comms were dead. She was on her own.

A pulsating timer superimposed on her vision grabbed her attention. Sixteen seconds to impact.

Adrenalin pumping through her veins and her hearts thumping in tandem, she issued the emergency exit protocol, escape her only thought. The cockpit would detach and propel her diametrically away from the potential hostile now just one hyat below.

No response. *Impossible.*

Nothing, no matter how many times she relayed the command. Her mind raced – there was nothing on this planet capable of compromising her species's technology. *So what the drokk was down there?*

She became aware of a turbulent sound permeating the edge of her hearing, followed by a slight vibration through her chair. Both sensations grew with each passing moment. The composite hull of the vessel began to creak and groan, as if under immense pressure.

Ten seconds.

Sinking back in her chair, resigned to her fate, she observed the monitor feeds from the cameras. One moment they displayed the murky greyish blue of the ocean depths; the next something shimmering and vast, circular in shape, previously unseen as if she had just passed through a field of camouflage much like that possessed by her ship.

No. Not possible.

Understanding dawned, which gave way to a feeling

of disappointment that consumed her entire being. Disappointment that her maiden voyage to the planet she had invested so much of her energy into, the planet that she had in some ways come to love, had to end with her demise. Disappointment that she could not show the humans how much more existed beyond their fragile comprehension. Disappointment that she could not save them.

With a final ironic smile, she crashed into the entity, isolated and alone.

*

Inside the heavily armoured bridge positioned at the pinnacle of a gargantuan hangar, Karulan examined the battered alien vessel. Initial data confirmed that, like the preceding unmanned drone, it was definitely not of native construction. The composite materials were orders of magnitude far more advanced than those created by the moribund population of Water Source 518, and he hadn't yet gained access to scrutinise the on-board tech. His drones had detected a possible lifeform contained within, which was something that needed to be dealt with tactfully. Intergalactic incidents between starfaring species were preferably avoided, especially given the xenophobic reputation his own kind had accrued. Rogue alien life forms – dead or alive – always presented a problem.

Taking a deep breath, he looked over at the shimmering giant portal from where the two ships had arrived. Enormous torrents of water were flooding inwards, billions upon billions of litres every hour, routed through the pipework, and the filtration system which had caught both craft.

Karulan knew he would be here for a while and almost contacted his wife to let her know before thinking better of it.

No point in poking the broulak; besides, Dephelle was enjoying herself with the kids on the nearest beach of their habitat, as were many others of their amphibious species. Five thousand kilometres in diameter and home to twenty billion souls, Loceramm was just one of thousands such megastructures scattered across the galaxy, each one full of oceans, seas and lakes. Every home, every workplace, every park; they all had at least one gratifying pool. The apparel worn by his kind had been designed to implement skin hydration, the designs becoming ever more flamboyant with each passing generation, and yet the powerful urge to blissfully submerge their smooth skin in cool, refreshing, open water was genetic, and ultimately impossible to deny.

While a suitable methodology for the mass creation of water existed, the logistics of sourcing, capturing, and combining the required elements burdened the process. It never ceased to amaze Karulan that despite the far-flung dominance of his species – both galactic and scientific – the discovery of planets with an abundance of water was a rare find indeed. The presence of a water intake portal was a great status symbol amongst the habitats; like all of Loceramm's residents, he was exceedingly proud that they continued with the time-honoured, elegant solution first devised so many centuries ago:

Simply steal it.

SEVEN PHOTOGRAPHS

BY HUW JAMES

A worn polaroid of a young woman holding a child is pulled out of a wallet that presumably serves no purpose other than holding memories.
  This thing's recording yeah?

The turning point for me was when our daughter came into the world. That's Erin and Saoirse just after they got out of the hospital. We were kind of reluctant to have a child of our own as we wondered if it was negligent of us to do so with the future they would have, and the impact that someone else consuming would cause to the environment. After looking into what seemed to be a wall of impossibility built around adoption, I relented. Only a year and a half later Saoirse was born. This was when I started to change.

I hadn't always been a "Doomer", obsessively lapping up anything negative about how things were heading, tracking all the subs on Reddit that would keep me informed about what was going wrong with pretty much everything, as far as I could tell. But it had become increasingly hard for me not to be. It was maddening how little most people seemed to care. The footballization of politics had driven a huge segment of the population into caring mostly about if their side was winning rather than whether anyone would benefit from the policies of who they "supported". With solutions to peak oil, new and exciting pandemics, and the catastrophic changes to our climate all requiring long term solutions with substantial long-term funding, no politicians had the appetite to commit to solving them. Anything outside the immediate election cycle was not worth focusing on, as the electorate would feel the pinch and blame them the next time they voted. With specific wedge issues being pushed to make everyone even further divided it was no wonder that by the time people were taking to the streets demanding a solution, it was far too late.

We were fairly well-off: I was working in the civil service managing a team of people handling claims. It was not overly exciting, but had a decent salary, a solid pension, and was safe. Erin did software development at a level I didn't really grasp covering "Front and Back end", which always made me giggle to myself. She brought in some serious money though, and with us both able to mostly work from home, it meant we were able to spend a lot of time with Saoirse.

In her first year, we decided to see if we could build our own home with sustainability in mind. Don't get me wrong, we loved our house up the coast, only a few minutes' walk to the beach, but it was on reclaimed land. We had been worried by articles showing we could be underwater in ten or twenty years. Fortunately, Erin was amazing at budgeting and putting money away for potential financial problems (things like the boiler going, car dying etc.), so we had pretty good savings, plus our house had appreciated considerably since we got our mortgage.

With inflation holding steady at a frankly offensive amount, and the never-ending supply chain issues making everything challenging (especially for those a lot more vulnerable than us), we decided if we didn't do it now, then it would never happen. So, we found a nice sized plot of land in a sheltered location, most importantly with groundwater, and met with an architect (and those guys are way more expensive than you imagine). It was quite a way out of the commuter belt, but the price was too good a trade-off for us. It did, however, mean we had to temporarily move in with my parents, something I hoped never to have to do again. They were extremely excited about having a grandkid though, and you can never turn down free childcare, even if it does mean we would be a bit cramped for a while. It also finally forced me to kick the smoking, as my mum wouldn't allow me in the house if I smelled of smoke. Thirty-four years old and getting told off by my mother, ha!

I really nerded out when we were planning the new house. I still wanted us connected to the grid (I wasn't that crazy), but I also wanted to make sure if in five, ten, twenty years and the shit completely hit the fan, that we could manage on our own. You know? Future proofing. Lots of solar panels, ground source heat pump, an actual well, a layout with passive cooling in mind, plenty of storage, low orbit satellite internet. Erin, of course thinking about things I hadn't even considered insisted we had a compost toilet put in downstairs in a second bathroom (not as smelly as they sound, but we still went mostly for plumbed-in). If things did go bad, she didn't want to be going outside in a latrine. My main concern was how long things like batteries would last. Would spares last in storage? How easy would it be for me to replace them? I started picking up books about trade skills, plumbing, home maintenance, etc. I took a few evening classes over the year and a bit it took to get everything ready for us to move in, while Erin or my parents took care of Saoirse. I needed to make sure that if anything went wrong, I would be in with a chance of fixing it myself at least.

*

He shows a picture of Erin in a large garden with a muddy toddler holding a small plastic spade, ton bags of soil or compost behind them.

After nearly two years of struggle in a weird, cramped situation living with the folks again, we were finally ready to move in. Saoirse was two now and speaking and stumbling around like an actual miniature human, and I was ready to get my gardening on. We had an insulated greenhouse with heating for overwinter, raised beds for vegs, and a few fruit trees (apples and pears, nothing exciting). I still went for a lot of decorative plants, as much native as I could do, but I couldn't live without Dahlias. Sure, they could be a bit of work before winter, but they were totally worth it.

*

He shows a picture of him proudly standing in front of a welded metal unit with wooden shelves, very rough industrial style to it.

I had gained a passion for making stuff out of wood and metal after an evening course the previous year, and a lot of reading, video tutorials, and an awful lot of mistakes. I wanted to see if I could make a run of it as a way of making a living. I agreed to stay in my job while I honed my skills in my little workshop space, and if it looked like I would be able to turn it into an actual paying job then I would go full time. Saoirse was six and moving into proper education by the time I was ready to make the move. We had found her a place in an Educate Together school about an hour's drive away. I would be taking her to and from school each day. I had concerns about the impact of driving a car this much – even an electric one, but we felt her education was more important.

Growing a decent amount of our own food was a huge boon to keep our cost of living down, while it was spiraling upwards for most people. There had been severe droughts in a lot of the countries Ireland imported some of our produce from, and that was just in Europe. Further afield, we were starting to see the second wave of environmental refugees. There were more conflicts over resources, and a few civil issues around the world in areas facing environmental pressure, sea-levels rising, water courses drying up (that massive river in Italy never flowed again), these kinds of things. With summers getting hotter, it was getting impossible to grow crops in many locations. You needed a lot more water when the temperature was even a couple of degrees warmer in growing season, and that was just not always possible. Many governments were beginning to rely even more on importing food, which was drastically driving up prices globally. This was unsustainable for many countries to afford, so people were starting to slowly migrate. Starving and poor, this was slow and ineffectual, but still made things even more challenging for nearby nations also feeling these affects. Ireland was still food secure for now, but with our exports now rising in demand, the price internally rose accordingly, and our poorest were being pushed to the edge.

*

He shows me a photo of Erin and Saoirse holding composite bows. Erin wearing a green Robin Hood style hat with a feather in it. Bow drawn back, a face of pure concentration.

When Saoirse was ten, we decided to move her to home schooling, something which was surprisingly easy to do now. A combination of rising population and poor future planning meant we were seeing unreasonably large classroom sizes. With both of us working from home, we felt it would be best to teach her at home and make sure she would get the attention she needed. I could work in the evenings and weekends around her learning, and we could make sure she was equipped to deal with a future that would need more practical skills. Erin was incredible in putting the majority of work into a syllabus and a schedule. We made sure to teach her the essentials of English language and literature, Maths, and a full spectrum of science. We also made sure she was learning electronics, plumbing, carpentry, and other areas related to construction and maintenance. We even had an archery tutor come over a couple of times a week to teach the three of us.

We felt it was important to closely follow the news with Saoirse to try to help her to understand the reasons behind what we were seeing. How people feeling the government had failed in addressing the cost of food and heating was once again pushing people to take to the streets. There were now occasional violent clashes with an ever more out of touch Garda, as well as talks of a general strike. Still, we were thankful that we were not in a place with trigger-happy armed police. We had seen some crazy footage from other nations.

*

He shows me a picture of Erin and Saoirse amidst a snowscape. Only the brown of the trees behind them, their branches dipping under the weight of snow, to mark they are at the base of a hill. With matching green parkas, they are dragging a small metal and wood sled behind them. Their faces are lit up with delight.

Saoirse was barely into her teens when we started to feel the changes more in Ireland. With years of escalation in ice melt in the north and arctic regions altering the mechanics of the ocean, the gulf stream had been slowed and disrupted along with the entirety of the AMOC also slowing down. This meant that our winters had started becoming significantly harsher. We were on the same latitude as the middle of Canada (you know where those massive hairy dogs are from), so whilst we had rarely hit zero in winter before, now we had long periods between minus five and minus ten. The government had barely bothered with helping insulate older housing stock over the past decade, and with heating costs skyrocketing for years, we were starting to see winters as a time of mourning, although we tried to enjoy it as much as we could, especially in the early days. The summers were a bit warmer at least, but dryer, we had a lot less rain now. Pools and use of hoses for decorative plants were permanently banned. Yes, I kept my Dahlias alive, even when I ran out of rainwater from the butts. The government were actually building a handful of desalinization plants to try and address the water issue. An island known globally for rain, and we didn't have enough of it anymore.

Despite the lack of rain and the cold winters, the main problem facing the country now was the storms. The past decade had been marked by a sharp increase in their frequency, but the severity now was magnitudes higher. It was no longer cost effective to repair power lines on the west coast, so more construction was required to move them all underground. There was a slow migration of people over to the east of the country and even across the water to the UK. As most of the storms coming from the Atlantic hit us first, they had lost most of their legs by the time they crossed the Irish Sea. The west and south-west of Ireland had been brutalized. The previous year, the entire landscape of a couple of counties on the west coast had changed. A three-month drought followed by two of the worst storms in memory in close succession had cleared away nearly all the topsoil from farms across the region. In less than a year a huge area of farmland was made barren.

A couple years on from this and protests and rioting were becoming commonplace. The armed forces had been deployed to aid the Garda on several occasions now. There were rumours of people intentionally getting themselves arrested to guarantee a roof over their heads, but there were no arrests at the protests, just baton charges and tear gas.

*

He shows a photo taken of Saoirse in a dark room lit only by the glow of the game on her monitor, slight reflection from posters on the wall.

We were still doing okay as a family for now. Mostly. Saoirse was feeling isolated. She was sixteen now, there was only one other family with someone her age nearby. We still had internet though and she was spending way too much time online chatting and gaming. The demand for online gaming had only increased further as things got worse. A small fee each month for an MMO would provide countless hours of entertainment and distraction.

Our home had been built to handle the weather changes: our location sheltered us from most of the winds, and the house physically protected the garden from the worst of it. We had great drainage for when we did get a period of heavy rainstorms, and we had enough insulation, cooling, and heating to cope with the hotter summers and colder winters. Occasionally we had issues with a system, but we could still get a specialist in if we couldn't manage it ourselves. I had entered full on survivalist mode a while back and had stockpiled lots of canned and packaged goods, gas cylinders for alternate fuel if we needed. I was convinced we were close to a full societal collapse, and wanted to make sure that above all, *we* would be covered. I mean when RTE stopped reporting on the riots that was a pretty solid sign that we weren't coming out of this.

*

He shows me a photo of him and Saoirse holding e-bikes with trailers attached to the rear of them both. Only he is smiling.

It was a bleak twentieth birthday for Saoirse. Her friend and her family had moved away to stay with family in the UK. She was desperate to head off to find somewhere with more people. Outside of our valley, a lot of the landscape was becoming barren, and we were no longer a food secure nation. There had been an influx of funding to attempt a move to climate-controlled greenhouses in the preceding years, but it had begun too late, and there was too much damage to them from storms. Our own greenhouse now looked pretty strange with part of it comprising of welded steel and plastic sheeting. Part of it had even been taken out by flying debris that also took down a portion of our boundary wall.

The internet was still operating on our satellite system, but was much less reliable, with a lot less information on it. Half of that was conspiracy nonsense as well. The world's falling apart, and people still take the time to blame lizard people. Anyway, that's when I started printing out the photos. I don't think I had used the printer for years. It still worked fortunately, and we still had a few sheets of photograph paper I could print some collages onto. During this time Saoirse and I were trading our expertise in building and repair for the few things we were low on to keep stocked up. Very rarely we would part with a book or two. I ended up losing a few beloved novels earlier in the year to get some tyres for the car that were still round and had tread. We only used the car if we were going further afield, and only to a spot nearby where we thought we wouldn't see anyone. When we were still getting regular news, there were reports of home invasions of "preppers" for their food stockpiles, so I was extremely worried that we would look like too much of a target with a fully charged and operational car.

It was only a few months later that we were forced to head further afield. Erin had developed a cough several months back. She was convinced it was the dry and dusty air, but even wearing a homemade mask when outside it had only gotten worse. Now in the past few days she had noticed lumps in her armpits. We were expecting the worst. We were certainly not equipped to deal with this, and with increasingly unreliable internet we were resorting to our own knowledge of the area and old paper maps to try and find someone who may be able to help. GPs, Hospitals, Clinics. Anywhere we may find someone to help with this situation.

We had bought two electric Toyota's about as late as we could still get them, which was a long time previously. One of them still had functional batteries at least. We kept it going by scavenging as needed from the other one for the rare occasions we headed out. The range wasn't as good as it used to be, so we were mostly driving around the nearest towns and villages desperate to find anyone to help. Most of these areas had been abandoned now and were beginning to look like old wild west movies with the wind blowing the dry, dusty ground. The only thing missing was the tumbleweed.

We had been out for a couple of days driving around and sleeping in the car, heading back to charge when we needed to. We were no longer caring about looking discreet. I was concerned about leaving Erin alone too long, and we had a lot of places to check within a fifty-kilometer circle. We had spoken to only a handful of people, mostly holding out in homes they had lived in most of their lives. Usually, they were people who grew a lot of their own food or had prepared well. None of them were thriving. All of them had stories about friends moving away, family begging them to come with them. In the end many of these people just wanted to live on their own terms, as it was more comfortable than risking the unknown and potentially worse conditions by moving.

We eventually found a lovely lady in her early fifties, who had worked as a Dental Nurse previously. She had heard from her visiting Son two years back that one of the hospitals in Dublin was still functioning. We could easily make it into the city on a full charge from home but would likely end up using the e-bikes and the trailer to go the final part. We would hopefully find something more specific on the way. We gave her what little we had with us and headed back home to charge the car overnight. We would leave first thing once it was light. Too much risk of hitting something on the roads at night.

*

It had been quite a journey just across the county, and we were still quite a way from the city. The roads were pretty terrible, and we had to stop to clear branches quite frequently. Trees and brambles, many of them dead, had encroached on both sides of the roads making them quite narrow. Barely passable for our knackered old Toyota. It was quite a sight as we crested the ridge to see a sign of civilization. Terracing on the hillside, something I had only seen in pictures before, and certainly not in Ireland. There was smoke coming from outside a former shopping center a mile or so down the road towards the edge of the town. The frames of the old steel-roofed, solid brick hardware and furniture stores had been repurposed into general shelters. The bones strong enough to handle the weather. Inside people had made homes and insulated them with materials from the nearby warehouses. Greenhouses bolted together in the carparks and braced to the south facing walls of the buildings were another way they were able to persist. A sizable group of people came out to meet us as we approached. They seemed very guarded but were able to confirm that Beaumont was reportedly still operational, and we should be able to reach it by nightfall. I must have missed something because Saoirse seems very keen on stopping there on the way back. We thanked them and headed on. If the motorway and roads were clear, we could be there in an hour.

*

Again, he holds up the polaroid of Erin and Saoirse as a baby.

I can't help but observe the extent to which Erin is different now, compared to the photo, lying in the bed opposite, attached to an IV and monitors. I know this is unfair: the photograph is over twenty years old.

So, is that ok? This is what you want, yeah? Have many come in with stories like this? What are you gonna do with these recordings anyway? It doesn't matter to be honest; it was just good to tell somebody, to have somebody listen. To feel for a moment that we made the right calls, that what we did mattered.

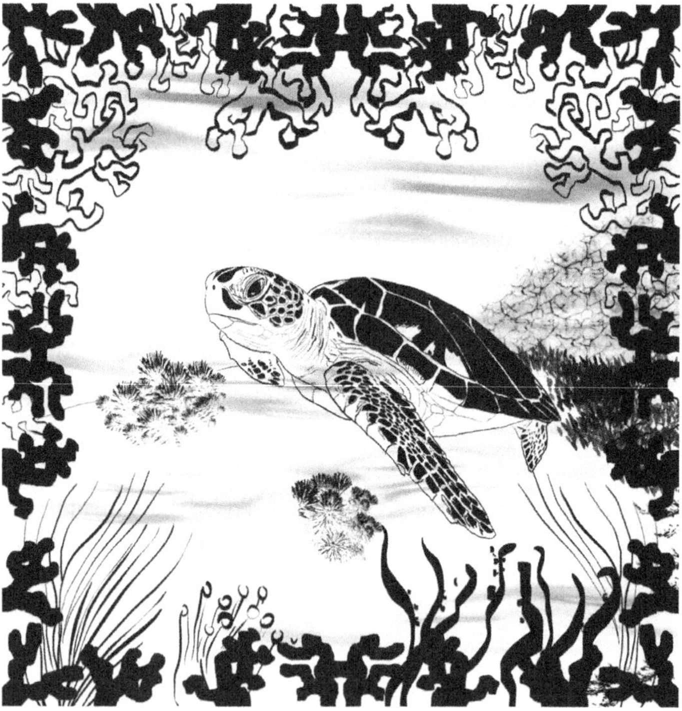

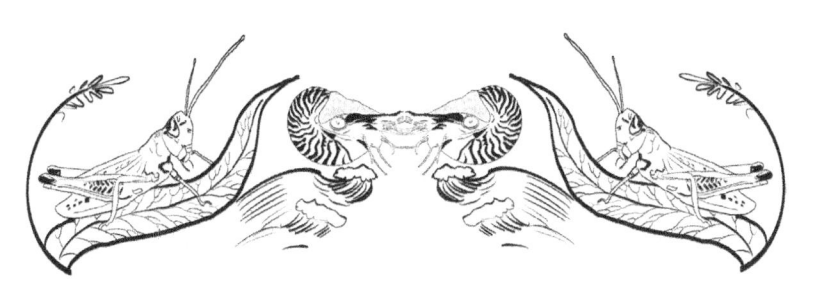

ANCIENT MEMORIES, ABOUT A VIRUS

BY GABRIEL WISDOM

I usually get lost in the most pleasant thoughts, planted in a canvas chair facing the sea. When my good friend, microbiologist Darwin 'Duke' Stadler, called, I activated 'face-time' and pointed the camera outward.

'Have a look, Duke.' The steep inner portion of a perfectly-shaped wave was breaking in controlled logarithmic spirals, like a liquid nautilus shell. I expected to hear about Fibonacci sequences or some other ideas delving into nature's perfect symmetry, but Duke had sobering news to share.

'Spencer,' he began seriously, 'you remember that paper describing five or six different parasites that hijack their hosts' brains, making them act horrifically?'

I mumbled, still fixated on the breaking wave, 'Mind-suckers, zombies, is that what you're talking about?'

'Right, zombie apocalypse. This is no joke,' he said emphatically. 'Ground parasites are common around lakes and streams, especially the tiny hairworms that infect land-dwelling insects like crickets. The little devils produce mind-controlling chemicals that, after dark, cause their cricket-hosts to crawl towards moonlight reflecting off of the water. The insect jumps in and drowns, while the hairworm feasts and shags until there are more hairworms.'

'Duke, you old romantic,' I smiled to myself, still wondering where this was headed.

'It gets worse, much worse.'

At this, I turned the phone's camera and noticed the dark circles under his eyes and swollen lids. 'Horsehair worms are harmless to vertebrates,' I said. 'If humans or other animals ingest the worms, they might experience a little stomach upset, but that's all.'

'This is different, Dexter,' he cautioned, using an old nickname from college. I preferred the more formal Poindexter, Doctor Spencer Poindexter. Then again, old friends can call you whatever they want.

'Duke,' I responded, thinking that was cooler than Dexter, 'considering how parasites help play a key role in regulating insect populations, the greater concern would be how climate change might upset this delicate balance. Organisms that make a living by sucking the life out of other organisms aren't necessarily bad. Without them, we'd be overrun with, umm, crickets, for example.'

There was a sharp crack in the air as another large wave was breaking over the reef. I watched my friend's cheeks fill with air, which he forcefully blew out. He leaned into the camera.

'Our mutual colleague, Janie Venter, visited me recently. She'd just returned from Hoh Rain Forest off Washington's Olympic Peninsula.' He stopped to draw another long breath. 'They found a new species of fungus, slightly different from the tropical parasite which infects carpenter ants. This one turns them into zombies. Clinically dead ants, walking.'

'Is she concerned about this new fungus among us?' I asked, trying to lighten the mood. It didn't help.

'Janie's more interested in what she accidentally discovered while digging in the melting permafrost, near Siberia.'

'Oh? What's that?' There was a long silence. I enjoyed people like Duke. Deep, critical thinkers who considered their words carefully. He was a genius, truly.

'They found a giant virus, about thirty thousand years old.'

'What do you mean by giant? How large?'

'You can actually see it with the naked eye.'

I gestured incredulously. A single virus is about one-thousandth of the width of a human hair.

He went on, 'So when Venter returned from Siberia with a sample for me to analyze, naturally I was excited. A prehistoric virus, for Christ sake!' The color was gone from Duke's face, and he was visibly irritated.

'Go on.'

'The bad news... the very bad news is that this virus, the virus in my laboratory, contains five hundred more genes than HIV, SARS, or COVID strains, which makes it far more dangerous.'

'And the good news?' I could feel my blood pressure rising.

'There isn't any.' Duke's eyes closed. 'The virus has been buried in oxygen-free ice, and it hasn't had a chance to spread and mutate, until now.' Then he looked up, barely whispering, 'The ice is melting.'

*

We stared at each other over the phone, and there was another sharp crack from a breaking wave at the outer reef. This time I didn't look, focusing instead on a cluster of dark blotches on

The Last Horizon

my friend's neck and face.

'Are you okay, Duke?'

'No, I'm not… This thing has… come alive.'

Thousands of capillaries appeared like little red dots. I thought I could see the effects of the virus traveling across his face. 'Duke!' I shouted, 'We've got to get you to a hospital!'

'No! Spencer, it's too late. Don't let anyone into my lab. Do you understand? No one must enter! I've sealed the doors with duct tape, and…'

Duke began to hack and cough. His eyes widened momentarily, and then froze open. 'Duke,' I shouted, 'Duke, stay with me!' He didn't respond.

*

At the time, I hadn't the presence of mind to use the facetime recording feature, but I do recall seeing those dark facial blotches turning red. I ran inside the house to get my keys. By this time, Duke looked catatonic, with his mouth open as though he'd seen an apparition. The only available phone was the one in my hand, and I didn't want to lose the connection, so I decided to drive to his laboratory at the University, about three miles from the beach. Just as I was about to turn the ignition, I glanced at the phone. The tiny red balls, those that I had taken for bursting capillaries, now had the appearance of spherical orbs studded with spikes. My heart beat faster and I could hear the blood pounding in my ears. The little spikes were proteins sticking out from the virus's fatty outer membrane. Just as my friend had described, the ancient virus was just large enough to see with the naked eye!

I pulled out of the driveway, and lost the connection with Duke's phone. 'Think,' I told myself, realizing I couldn't just call the police or paramedics. This was too complex, and no one would have believed a story about a giant virus.

I dialed Janie Venter.

'Hey Spencer,' she purred gently through a thick French accent. 'How's my boy?' Janie and I had dated briefly in college before she'd met her first husband. A nice guy, I had decided. Actually, I liked every one of her husbands, all five or six of them, it was hard to keep track.

'Janie, I need your help. It's about Duke. He's at the lab. That virus of yours seems to have infected him. He's…'

She completed the sentence. 'Self-quarantined? Is that right?'

I explained in rapid detail what had happened, including the spherical spiked orbs covering his face. 'Duke said that your Siberian virus contains more genes than HIV, SARS, and COVID.'

'Merde!' Janie blurted.

'Any suggestions? Thoughts, ideas, anything?' I pleaded.

'Duke's going to be okay, sort of.'

'What the f–'

'Hold on a minute!' she insisted. 'What you saw happen to Duke, well, the same thing happened to me. They say I was sick for nine days, but I have no recollection of that time, other than the very strange, very frightening dreams. I'm fine now, except for the dreams.'

Janie told me she'd been infected shortly after interring the virus from the ice. Her Siberian guide had brought her to his cabin in a village outside Bratsk. The man, his wife, and their two children had been previously infected, and consequently had built up a natural immunity. It turned out that everyone in and around the Irkutsk Region had been exposed and had recovered. There was one lingering side-effect. She said the virus seemed to have tapped into ancient genetic memories, passed down in the DNA from our earliest ancestors.

*

'I'll take Duke home to my place until he's better,' she reassured me.

'The dreams, Janie. You say they're strange and frightening. What do you mean?'

'Ah, well, there's a recurring falling dream. I'm living in the trees with other, um, I guess you'd call them primates...'

*

Eventually, Darwin "Duke" Stadler recovered, just as Janie Venter had promised. What I soon learned was that the virus had begun spreading before Stadler knew he'd been exposed. At some point, I'm not sure when, I became sick, recovering mostly, with the exception of the recurring nightmares, much like those Janie described.

These days, I'm preoccupied with the scientifically-debated concept of genetic memory. The idea is that we all have a family lineage of survival embedded in our DNA. These genetic imprints are inherited from ancestors who survived long enough to successfully mate, passing those memories along at their prodigy's conception. Those who hadn't mated were simply not adding new data to the genetic memory bank. While not directly coded in DNA, these expressions are nonetheless real hand-me-downs. Prior to now, there has been no verifiable evidence that human beings possessed the ability to somehow activate recollections that once belonged to their ancestors. We all need to sleep and, unfortunately, I have found there is no escape from the frightening horrific memories.

The Last Horizon

✷

Most nights, I find myself living among a group of prehistoric hominids who are human-like but not Homo Sapiens. My 'family' stays in the trees. We don't have words but manage to communicate via a series of chattered sounds and crude gestures. Our clan is different from those that occupy the ground caves. Fights occur most nights over food and territory.

In one particularly vivid and recurring nightmare, I am being pushed from my loft, losing balance, and falling. Desperately clutching at branches on the way down, there's a realization that I'm going to die or, worse, that I'll be crippled. Others from the clan who'd fallen and couldn't get up, were dragged off by one of the large cats. Fortunately, I land on a spot of soft wet ground, but then I've got to survive among the hostile and very aggressive cave folk. The dream ends with what I assume is a female hominid. We're hiding together in a rocky crevice. I'm aware of the pronounced low forehead and a large pelvis. She stares at me with a robust jaw, and the last thing I remember is the warm caress of fingertips.

THE COW

BY JAMIE BEAR

It was unprovoked. Some may argue that the length of her skirt and the thickness of her lashes were encouraging, but we're not in bible times. She stared down at her balloon of a stomach, rain pouring against the window, battering the cheap fibreglass panes: entrapped by nature's wrath and the judgement that she felt she encountered whenever she stepped outside. It wasn't a choice she was given, and many imparted their opinion like they were stating the obvious, without giving it a second thought. Raised a Catholic in an Irish community, it didn't matter that her location had changed; her mind remained loyal by force to those who lovingly raised her. Also, she loved this baby. Whilst the start had been confusing and she'd felt as though her body was being pulled from underneath her, she'd made peace with her new little friend and vowed only to love them. Never would she let the circumstance of their creation dampen her love. If anything, she saw it as a gift from God, a companion when the world felt so bleak.

She caressed her stomach and gazed through the slit in the

curtains at a pigeon perching on the picket fence. Around her lay an open box of cereal, three mugs full of cold un-drunk tea and a copy of *Pride and Prejudice* decorated with delicate tear stains. She knew there would be no Darcy for her but there was hope to be found in this new life she harboured.

At age six she wanted to be a dancer. All of her friends would practise flicking their legs into the air on the playground, feet permanently positioned like a ballerina. At age nine she decided that actually she'd rather be a firefighter and save cats from trees. She loved cats. Then when secondary school started, she thought she might like to be a teacher so she could marry Mr. Jackson. He taught History and was 'oh so dreamy', but then he gave her a detention for talking too much in year eight and so she abandoned that idea and moved her ambition onto 'Reality TV star'. She was normal. A normal kid with big ideas full of absolutes and dreams. The world that surrounded her, although far from perfect, was all she'd known, and she was content. When you read about these stories in the news, hearing of 'that girl that was raped', we don't stop to consider the normality of her life beforehand and how she can never return to that. Often we say that we sympathise, that we can only imagine how hard it must be. Yet, secretly, or not so secretly in some cases, we make judgements that eventually rule us, egged-on by vices and desires such as greed, status and money. We forget what really matters and are overruled by a longing for more. We become accustomed to the idea that we deserve what we want. She too once felt like this, the beauty that comes with being young, believing the world is your oyster. Now, each day was a journey she had no choice but to get through. If she could choose to, she'd kill herself. But now it wasn't just her, continuing was the only option left.

She also hated the misery she had succumbed to, she hated being so eternally pessimistic. Often, she tried to turn it around and naturally, there were moments when her mind would wander from her circumstance, and she'd find herself smiling. Books, films, the mindlessness that accompanied daytime TV, all of these provided moments of respite. She was sentient, and nothing is ever perpetually awful. Plus, there are moments of happiness in ignorance, for ignorance is bliss to those who are blessed with it. She tried to smile more, enjoy the small things like the dawn chorus, a perfect cup of tea, and a packet of bourbon biscuits. As long as you live in a way that isn't hurting others, what more can you aim for than happiness?

*

It was three weeks before her due date and she waddled more than walked but she was grateful just to know someone was there. She'd cut her parents off a few weeks after she'd found out she was pregnant and that left her feeling lonelier than ever. They'd insisted that she kept it and unsubtly implied that there must have been something to provoke her attacker. They didn't explicitly say it was her skirt or her boots or her low-cut top, but it wasn't difficult to read between the lines. She needed to make the decision herself and so she'd stopped returning her mother's increasingly petulant phone calls. When she decided to keep her baby, she'd let them know but decided that regardless of her decision, she needed only to be heard, not advised. It'd now been two months since she'd had a proper conversation with either of them. She was lonely but she knew she wasn't alone in her situation. Millions of women are raped, it's not something that just happened to her. Besides, there was no point dwelling on the moments of her past that brought her no happiness. She knew all she could do was move forwards.

*

In the early hours of a Wednesday morning her son was born. She was, naturally, completely in love and for the following few days she didn't sleep, just watching him, constantly listening for the sound of his breathing. She named him George, inspired by her love for Austen, she knew he'd grow to be a proper and kind man. She did wonder though what It would be like raising a boy when she knew nothing about them. She had two sisters and her father was a man she most definitely did not wish to replicate. She feared what he would become and what sort of life he would wish to lead.

*

Over the next week, the new family got into a routine, and she looked for support outside of home. After research, she'd found support groups for women like herself and drove sixteen miles on the second Tuesday of the month for her first session. The room was full of chatter as she entered through the double doors with George in clutch. She knew it was silly but she wanted to impress him: show she could make a great life for the two of them. In any case, having him there encouraged her to be confident amongst this new group of women. Taking a seat next to a tall fair lady in her mid to late twenties, she introduced herself to the group. The older lady opposite her smiled and encouraged her to open-up. There was no need for small talk and meek introductions, they'd all been through it. Slowly, she began to tell her story; how she felt suffocated by her parents, by society to comply to the 'rules' set out for young women. She told how he forced her and how she tried to call for help but it was late and no one stopped. How she felt silenced, how she couldn't understand why no one cared enough to ignore the taboos that cloud the world. The more she spoke the more confident she felt, validated by the presence of the warriors who sat in this circle on a Tuesday evening.

The lady to her right then began to tell her story. She had long red hair and a black duffle bag perched on her lap. She'd had her daughter out of a sexually abusive encounter and explained that she'd been too afraid to confront her feelings until she began these classes. She talked about how scared she was every day that her little girl was entering an endless cycle, one that won't end because not enough people care. A cycle that won't end because there are too many monsters in this world. The session concluded and George was carried into the car, close to his mother's chest, her hands supporting his tiny head as she put him into the baby seat. Although draining, she finally felt a sense of camaraderie. She wasn't alone.

Arriving home, she pulled up to the house to be greeted by a stiff man in a light grey suit. Her guard went up immediately and she still felt intimidated alone in male presence. Although it was something she was aware she needed to move past, raising a son especially, she still felt nervous. Taking George out of the car she introduced herself. Instantly the atmosphere was stifling. She knew something was wrong as he invited himself inside.

'We've had suggestion to believe you're an unfit mother. Your son isn't safe with you. Do you think it's appropriate to take your son to an environment of that nature?'

She was in disbelief. What environment? A room full of gentle kind-hearted women? She felt cold, once again the world was taking all it could from her but she knew she couldn't let this go without a fight. She asked how he dare suggest she's unfit, where were the authorities when she was raped? Was it insufficient evidence or turning a blind eye? She assured this man that her son was safe and loved and cared for, that there was no place better for him than with his mother. A tear rolled down her cheek and sat above her lips. She held him as close as she could for this couldn't be real; they couldn't take him away. The man took photos of the kitchen on his phone. He took pictures of the spot on the bed where she'd put his sleep suit.

'He sleeps with you?'

A man questioning her skills as a mother, her choices, like he'd ever had to question whether or not he could afford to buy organic linen bedding. She'd never crush him, he slept on her chest, he was part of her. There was no way she would ever do any damage; he was as much her heart as the organ itself.

'We have cause to believe you're not fit right now.'

She protested. It didn't work. She fought, it made it worse. He said the next morning someone would collect her son and that she would have supervised visits if she wanted. She could fight in court. He closed the door behind him and she folded into herself with George against her chest and sobbed.

*

The following morning was harrowing. She hadn't moved all night other than to feed her son. She couldn't let him go knowing in a few short hours he'd be taken from her for good. He was wearing a pale blue baby grow with a small bear on the front and a pair of knitted booties she'd made towards the end of her pregnancy. He'd had hiccoughs all night and she'd only just got him settled when the knocks at the door reverberated through the floorboards. George cried. He knew what was happening, she could feel it. She pleaded as soon as she opened the door, but it was like they didn't care. Her social position and her gender both weighed as heavy burdens in her case and she knew that societal change wasn't imminent. If anything the world felt like it was going backwards. They took him from her arms and she begged and begged but it didn't matter for she knew she was nothing to them but a woman. As the hours alone went by her milk leaked and the pain grew stronger, but she needed something to stay close to him. She needed everyone to know she had a son. In the night she cried out for her George, but no one came and no one cared. She was a woman.

Her purpose had been fulfilled.

*

You may question why there is a short story about rape and gender inequality in a collection inspired by climate change. It's important to draw a parallel between providing the facts and telling a story someone will willingly engage with. Although this is a story, the reality for a dairy cow is of a likeness to the short you have just read. Dairy cows are artificially inseminated and their calves are taken from them at birth. Often you can hear the female cows calling for their babies, yet as a society we continue to consume dairy products and eat veal without any thought of the origin of those products, or the suffering that was necessary to produce them. Why shouldn't we feel similar empathy for the animal kingdom to that which we feel for people. Or rather, if we do feel empathy, why does society tell us not to be sympathetic or compassionate? We separate mother from baby for material gains and ignore the pain we cause to beings who are sentient in the same way that humans are.

Concern for animal welfare and climate change are also very closely related. The dairy industry contributes around 3.4% of global CO_2 emissions.[21] To put this into perspective, that is more than double the amount created by aviation. In South America, 71% of deforestation has been driven by demand for animal products. The amount of land needed to fulfil the demand for red meat is destroying the Amazon with 700,000 square kilometres of the rainforest being destroyed since 1970. Stopping your intake of animal products will not only allow the animals to live fulfilling, long lives but also is suggested as the "single biggest way" by Oxford University that we can reduce our carbon footprint, shrinking it to 73%[22]. One plant-based meal choice can save the same amount of carbon emissions it takes to drive a car across the UK and switching to a vegan diet will massively reduce your own carbon footprint. If lots of people choose to do it, we can really help to avert dangerous climate change AND create a world with far less suffering for the animal kingdom.

---

[21] BBC news article from 2020: 'Where better to start than dairy: in 2015, the industry's emissions equivalent to more than 1,700 million tonnes of CO2 made up 3.4% of the world's total of almost 50,000 million tonnes that year. That makes dairy's contribution close to that from aviation and shipping combined (which are 1.9% and 1.7% respectively).' https://www.bbc.com/future/article/20201208-climate-change-can-dairy-farming-become-sustainable

[22] Independent article: https://www.independent.co.uk/lifestyle/health-and-families/veganism-environmental-impact-planet-reduced-plant-based-diet-humans-study-a8378631.html

AT FIRST BITE

BY STEPHEN BEESON

At Midnight on 24 December 2035, the last human being on the face of planet Earth died. This ostensibly auspicious event was anything but: he just stopped breathing whilst in an alcohol induced coma. One couldn't blame him for being drunk. He'd found some rather nice Chateau Latour 2017 on one of his long walks, which he drank on returning to his isolated farm in Provence to mask the disappointment of once again not meeting anyone on his travels and to try and dispel the intense feeling of loneliness.

Unaccustomed to the delights of alcohol, the wine blurred his senses and raised his mood for a little while before the depression returned even deeper than before. He desperately opened and consumed bottle after bottle until he passed out. Three days later the end came and John Smith, who had left England some fifteen years before to find peace and solitude in rural France, expired having found that solitude enforced brings no comfort at all.

The Last Horizon

*

It had been a close thing as to who would be the last. Were angels of a mind to gamble, the sensible money would have been on the Buddhist monks in Tibet, situated as they were in an isolated monastery high in the mountains, providing a likely candidate. But when a passing yeti – who had picked up the virus that had caused the demise of humankind lower down the mountains – infected the yaks which provided the monks with milk and cheese, the favourites fell at the last fence.

The virus had frequently mutated after its original appearance some ten years previously, at a New York hot dog stand during One Direction's fourth final World Tour, all made possible by hypersonic aeroplanes that meant that they could play in Sydney, Paris and New York all in the same day. The changes often occurred just as a cure was tantalisingly close. Crossing the barriers between humans and animals, both equally succumbing to its ravages, no species on the planet was immune to the killer's onslaught, with the exception of the New Zealand Kiwi, which revelled in the returning isolation. Eventually, even insects were affected. This was to prove the undoing of one group of Jewish ascetics who at the first news of the pandemic-that-would-end-all-pandemics disappeared into the desert to eat locusts and honey.

Not that a cure would have brought a halt to the progress of the mutating microscopic murderer; it had taken a long time for the doctors and scientists to establish that there was a virus responsible for the sudden increase in unexplained deaths. This was in part due to the fact that there were no symptoms, no sign of illness until suddenly after a loud burp people just collapsed with a faint smell of onions pervading the body (rumours abounded that it was a sulphurous odour, a sure sign of either the devil's work or anal flatulence, but this was soon poopooed!),

Food poisoning, obesity, climate change, sedentary lifestyles were all blamed until a super-fit English cricket team expired at the same time during the final test in Melbourne with Australia 300 runs behind in their second innings with only 1 wicket left and a full day's play remaining. Victory would have retained the Ashes for England. The Australian captain claimed victory and had just managed to grab the small urn and a tinny before his own final expulsion of stomach gasses.

Newspapers and the rest of the media (mainstream or otherwise) competed to find a name for the virus. The French called it the 'New English Disease'. In England the reaction to this was to call it 'French Flu', for a time with speculation that it had been brought into the country by illegal immigrants from Calais before it became known as the 'Boche Bug' as a result of the rumour that it had been developed by Nazi scientists and had escaped from Porton Down as a result of Government cutbacks. The World Health Organisation not to be outdone called it 'Panvirus 001' but that never really caught on.

Alternative cures for the virus started to abound in the press and on the internet. The entire world supply of vinegar was used up in the first few months of 2026 as the old perennial found a new desperate audience. Copper bracelets enjoyed a similar renaissance. Not to be outdone the Chinese reinvented acupuncture by making the needles radioactive. Homeopaths came up with three drops of essence of spring onion a day on food. 'Magic Mushrooms' achieved worldwide popularity and were sold on the internet either dried or in kit form. This fell into disrepute when unscrupulous vendors substituted various poisonous toadstools when supplies of the mushroom were spent.

A report stating that 5 cc of semen freshly extracted from a male infected with the virus would, if taken daily, provide the taker with immunity. Instantly badges were produced for men to wear stating 'I am Infected'. Men wearing these badges proudly went out into the community awaiting the inevitable approach from members of both sexes. One poor postman was kidnapped and held in a convent for twenty days before he eventually succumbed.

Of course, the virus was not directly responsible for all the deaths, with suicides, both deliberate and unintentional, becoming the second highest cause of mortality as mass depression set in. The bill-boarded messengers of doom with their "The End of the World is Nigh" found themselves victims of angry passers-by who despised them for being smart-arses and used the billboards to batter them to an early extinction. The crew of a US nuclear submarine on patrol in the Arctic decided collectively to launch its Kraken nuclear missiles under the North Pole to celebrate the 4th of July in style.

The entire remaining population of San Marino marched on the Vatican in order to bring the Pope John Paul XXXIX to book for declaring himself a homosexual, only to find that the Swiss Guard had upgraded from pikes to machine guns and flame throwers.

Bizarrely people stopped swimming with dolphins and started swimming with sharks and walking with sheep, the latter on isolated mountain tops where reverting to their comedic past they threw themselves off shouting 'they don't so much fly as plummet,' proving unequivocally that Monty Python really did get the last laugh.

Beachy Head became a holiday destination as Butlins set up camp there albeit for a short time as the Redcoats couldn't keep their smiling personae alive for long and became jumpers themselves.

Reality TV shows blossomed again as people became even more desperate for their fifteen minutes of fame in the increasingly short window of opportunity left open to them. A particular favourite was 'Fastest Gun' using live ammunition, followed by 'Extreme Arctic Circle Strip Poker'.

Popular, if somewhat historically inaccurate, American Civil War Battle reconstructions accounted for a high number of deaths. This was revised by British, Belgian, and French TV companies who banded together to produce "Waterloo" where twinned towns would compete along the lines of 'It's a Knockout' to re-enact the famous battle with live period weapons, including cannons. The French soon tired of this when the English kept playing their joker by bringing in a Prussian town they had become twinned with. The Americans meanwhile tiring of their own series introduced 'Alamo, the revenge' to their networks.

Most successful of all was 'You're a celebrity and you're staying' which managed to decimate the number of C (and below) list celebrities, and a revamp of 'Big Brother' which gave the FBI the remit to ensure all house disputes were settled peacefully, WACO style.

On a macro scale, economies and governments collapsed together. The moral fabric that kept neighbour from killing neighbour, just because he had planted Leylandii in their garden or allowed their cats full roam to defecate in yours, disintegrated. As alcohol and drug supplies dried up, unprotected sex became the pleasure of choice and STDs spread like wildfire.

Deep in a Kremlin bunker, following the discovery by Russian scientists that the virus was vulnerable to high levels of radiation, the remaining members of the Politburo hatched the plan to eradicate it by launching their nuclear missiles at China and the US, in order to start the World War that could paradoxically save the human race. The plan backfired when having given the order to their nuclear silos to launch they discovered that their isolated operatives had changed the destination codes to Moscow as a protest for not having received their vodka rations for six months.

During this period of madness there were of course countless acts of kindness and bravery as humanity struggled to come to terms with its imminent demise and battled against the growing forces of evil. Many were still bolstered by their religions, the Jews and Christians united in their belief that the Messiah would now come, albeit for either the first or second time.

And then there was silence.

Newspaper presses ceased to roll, broadcasters went off air and the internet wound down as power companies around the world gave up the struggle to produce electricity. Hospitals closed, armies and police went home and stayed there. People waited for the inevitable.

*

John Smith was blissfully unaware of all of this. Self-contained in his small holding, he didn't shop anymore, he never took a newspaper and didn't have a radio, television or computer. He didn't have electricity or gas, and he burned wood from his own copse for heat. He had long since stopped going to the shop in the small village near his smallholding, tired of the local children throwing stones and abuse at him and of their parents who would usher their children home frightened of the mad Englishman. For years he had kept himself to himself, people frightened him.

He had been frightened as a child, by aged domineering

parents who expected him to subjugate himself to their wishes and become their carer, by the other pupils who laughed at him and derided him for just being different. When his parents had died whilst he was just eighteen, he used the money they had left to try to endear himself to his peers. For a while this was successful in that he joined a circle that invited him as long as he paid. He then made the mistake of trying to endear himself unsuccessfully to the girlfriend of the pack leader. Under his instigation they all set upon him and – bruised internally and externally – he sold his house and moved to France.

The locals had a deep mistrust of the odd 'Étranger' in their midst, which suited John; no one tried to befriend him and he was left very much to his own devices. He went for long walks in the countryside avoiding, where he could, any human contact. It was during these long walks that he eventually realised that there was now no longer anyone to avoid. Wildlife too had seemed to vanish.

It was on one specific walk past a large chateau, where he had occasionally hidden in nearby trees to watch the comings and goings, that he noticed the garden, previously so pristinely kept, was now running wild. Cars had not moved from where they had been parked since his last visit some twelve months before; the same doors were left open, and the building exuded an air of abandonment.

Summoning up his courage he ventured into the property. Moving from room to room, he found this once proud building had been deserted. Expensive paintings hung from the wall were now covered with dust, with no eyes to observe them save his. The dining table showed the remnants of a meal as frugal as the ones to which he was accustomed. The only difference being the empty wine bottles on the table. Children's toys lay scattered around several of the bedrooms. A rocking horse stood proudly in the corner of the nursery patiently awaiting a rider that would never come. Every room told him that this house no longer had occupants and had not for some time. On an impulse he went down into the cellar. The coldness chilling his bones, he selected half a dozen bottles of wine which he placed into the shoulder bag that he always carried with him on his walks.

He went home with a sense of guilt at his theft and watchful as his crime may have been observed, by whom he did not know. On his arrival home, despite his trepidation he chose to walk into the village, for once down the main street. The houses showed the same degree of abandonment as the Chateau. He was alone.

Returning home, he ransacked his kitchen to find the corkscrew which had been unused for years. He started to drink.

*

As the air in John Smith's lungs was exhaled for the last time, Eve opened her eyes wide in astonishment as she struggled to take in what she had just witnessed: the entire history of humanity with its whimpered ending.

She looked down at the apple in her hand, perfect but for the one bite she had taken, the flesh still white against the deep red of the skin. A tear started to form in her eyes, the first she had ever known as her ears picked up the urging repetition 'Share it with Adam.'

She looked up to the branch above her where the serpent was languidly coiled and experienced another first: an intense feeling of anger which grew as the monotonous sibilant voice continued.

The snake, bored by the sound of his own voice and impatient at the lack of response from Eve, yawned. This proved to be its second mistake. Eve pushed the apple into the gaping chasm. The serpent coughed and spluttered but could not dislodge the fruit, so deep had Eve plunged it. It fell writhing to the ground. Eve, horrified by all that had happened, ran off shouting for Adam, for the comfort that he would provide her.

God smiled at all They had witnessed and lowering Their hand removed the apple from the now desperate snake, who slithered off into the undergrowth and out of the garden. God knew that Eve would not tell Adam any of what she had seen, as Adam, a man, would not really be able to take any of it in. God also knew that having given humans free will, they and their descendants would make mistakes, as Eve had made the first when she tasted the apple, but that the ending for humanity would not be what Eve had witnessed. For now, rooted in the depth of their being, there was a glimmer of understanding: it is never too early to take a different path.

A DAY

BY AMIE ANGÈLE BROCHU

The air was different today. It was thinner, warmer and full of tension, like there was an anticipation of something about to happen. Tym knew these shafts and corridors like no other, an engineering marvel that had stood the test of time. The heated, dry air moved past him as he stood silently, briefly interrupting his work. Typically, the cooler drafts of the sub-levels were a welcome respite from the heat of the upper decks, but today no such relief was to be found. As the warm, dry wind drifted through the corridors, Tym felt the moisture stir on his back and a sense of unease washed over him.

The signs had been mounting for some time. The air currents in the shafts were changing. Everything was heating up. The corridors were drier, with the water reserves approaching critical. His biweekly reports were showing quantifiable declines, a pattern that he'd observed with other systems. Despite recycling ninety percent of all waste, the reprocessing scientists had yet to put forth a solution. At the previous council meeting Tym had proposed increased insulation to the upper decks with heat proof shielding to maintain the humidity levels, but his request had been denied. The precious resources were needed elsewhere. Despite Tym's mounting frustration there was little he could do. The general agreement among the colony was that uncontrollable events were occurring around them, making his people feel increasingly helpless and vulnerable to these incremental changes.

For Tym, maintaining the ventilation shafts was a daily affair in which he spent most of his time as a structural engineer. It was dim and tight in the corridors, but it was the type of work that suited him. For, as social as he tended to be, he still preferred his own company and the solitary work in the shafts fuelled this need. Unlike his friends and co-workers, he was deeply introspective and the monotonous repetitive tasks allowed him to visit the spaces in his head more frequently. He enjoyed maintaining the shafts, visiting the labyrinthine bends and curves, much like the tunnels of his mind. They were a familiar place; safe, shrouded in darkness, yet purposeful, maintaining separation and dividing off sections. Alone he would travel up and down the various levels, performing his specialised duties, sensing the hustle and bustle of the rest of his people beyond the walls of the passageways. Everyone was going about their lives and daily tasks, but paying little heed to Tym.

He climbed through a narrow opening and into one of the main corridors. He needed to go to the next section seven levels above which hadn't been visited for several days. Tym decided to take a shortcut through one of the Great Halls. Unlike most of his kin, he preferred to keep walking long distances to a minimum. Being larger meant that he had a harder time getting around. There were times when he envied his petite, lithe friends, yet he knew his size was what got the attention of the most beautiful woman, Queen Reyes of House Volar, and was most likely the reason why she'd become his wife.

One would think marriage to the Queen would be like taking the express elevator to higher status and privilege, and yet here was Tym, a king in name only, status unchanged, maintaining ventilation shafts. Certainly there'd been other suitors similar in size to him. Few, but suitable, nonetheless. When they dined in their quarters alone, Tym now and then wondered what she'd seen in him to begin with. Perhaps it was his pale complexion, sometimes translucent in the light or his quiet, calm demeanour. He never bothered asking her, for fear her answer would deflate his anticipated response. Although there were high fertility rates amongst his people, female births were few; therefore, being a male meant rejection was an ever-present risk, and even the most outstanding man could face bachelorhood indefinitely.

As Tym thought of his wife, her soft round face drifting through his mind, he made his way through the corridors into the Great Hall. It wasn't much of a room or anything grand as the name suggested: rather, it was a hollowed-out area full of memories; remnants of past territorial battles with other colonies and relics of their shared diasporic experiences filled the space. To walk here was to reflect on their history. The Elders were his people's memory, proffering stories of how their society had faced so many adversities throughout their survival. His long-lived wife was among them, although she spoke little of her experiences. The most recent territorial war, the Battle of Mato, had forced them to move yet again not too long ago. The defeat was still etched in Tym's mind. Since the conflict the fear of another war had become prominent within his concerned thoughts for the soldiers as they trained and maintained their silent observation posts. Nothing but loss came out of these hostilities.

As a child, Tym had heard tales of various skirmishes at their borders, as foreign colony scouts had sought provisions to supplement their own dwindling resources. Tym recalled very little about the outside world before the Battle. In times past, safety was rarely an issue, due to the remote and secluded location of their colony. Exploring the realm beyond the thick reinforced walls of his home, Tym's earliest memory had been of his passing by shallow pools of fresh water with his friends. Looking up, he'd been mesmerized by the immense branching towers that sheltered him and his companions from the burning sun. However, the Battle offered a stark reminder that under these rapidly changing skies, safety was no longer guaranteed. The search for food, water and other supplies meant venturing farther away from home and the increased risk of entering another colony's territory.

Most colonists believed that they would have won the fight if not for the Termita Pox virus that had infected half their kin. Tym, like many others in his colony, had noticed that infections had been growing in frequency in recent times. There were never before seen illnesses thriving in the changing atmosphere within the colony, bringing mysterious sicknesses that continually baffled their doctors. No one was exempt from the suffering and quick death. Children, adults and elderly alike were at risk because of the changing environment. The growing frequency of illnesses was a constant fear, increasing their vulnerability in ways for which they could never prepare.

Tym had been a young boy at the time, barely out of the nursery, and he could still recall the day the invasion had taken place. It had been sudden, in the middle of the night, with such brutality and swiftness there'd been little to no warning. Their defences had been overwhelmed because so many were ill and dying. Adults staggering under the misery of crippling fever and bodily weakness had taken to the fight, giving their last ragged breath to protect their home. Queen Reyes has led their colony into battle, a fierce fight, one which had made her a widow. Reyes never liked to speak of her first husband out of respect for his memory and as a form of self-preservation from reliving the trauma of his loss. Tym understood her need all too well, being quiet and reserved about many personal matters himself.

As Tym felt the warm dry air around him, he knew his wife faced another fight; one on a completely different plane. This was an assault where they could not survive by tactical planning and overpowering opponents with brute strength. This encounter was invisible and unpredictable. They faced an unnamed foe that threatened their very existence by attacking their mechanisms of daily survival. The air quality and availability of food was diminishing, affecting the health of all of Tym's people. There were some days that all the soldiers did was carry the dead to the cemetery pits. There was no means of escape, only adaptation. Tym knew such adjustments would bring more death and destruction as he worried about the future.

Many of the Elders spoke of times when the seasons had been predictable, when the rains had come and the sun had shone. But now, things were very different, with rains that would not come and heat that sucked the moisture from every leaf and root leaving, brittle scorched land in its wake. The Elders knew very little of the reasons for these changes, but devastating they were. Life for Tym and his people had been interrupted by forces out of their control. Queen Reyes sought answers on how to better prepare, but the answers weren't forthcoming.

Tym continued down another corridor, entering the upper shafts where the air was now hotter and drier. He paused briefly in the dimness and waited. Something wasn't right. The air was wrong. He felt fear wash over him. Tension made his body rigid. He felt the wall, noticing the vibrations growing more intense. The activity in nearby corridors grew more frantic. Then he noticed the smell of something acrid, something like smoke. Smoke? Tym's confusion escalated. The alarm sounded. A threat was eminent. He needed to get to his Queen.

Emerging out of another narrow opening he was almost knocked off his feet as a platoon of red-helmeted soldiers brusquely moved past him. His close friend Vance might be among them, but the dimness of this section and his relatively poor eyesight prevented Tym from picking him out in the group. The chaos was commencing. More soldiers rushed past. He moved along the side of the corridor, the heat and smoke growing. It was becoming harder to breathe. He could feel the fear, panic and confusion. He saw groups of people cram themselves into the shelter tubes, hoping to escape the unknown threat. Tym was not brave, but he was not going to abandon his people or his Queen. This self-professed bachelor was a newly made King and he was going to prove himself worthy to the colony and his new bride.

Tym moved down the various levels, through the ensuing pandemonium. His large size made manoeuvring a challenge as the corridors and shafts filled with frantic people carrying infants and goods as they passed him. He squeezed through another narrow entryway and grunted. Never once had he been so annoyed at his size, but today in his urgency to get to his wife, he found it the most cumbersome thing. In his own urgency and unidirectional focus he took a wrong turn and ended up in the Gardens. He stopped, noticing the large, manicured plots abandoned. The rows and mounds of the mushroom beds were left unattended. One of the colony's preferred nutritional delicacies, usually tended with great care, was left exposed, vulnerable. His people were known experts in fungiculture as a food source. Tym recalled the time when he'd been younger and had tried his hand at tending the fungal mounds.

Unfortunately for Tym, there'd been nothing green about his thumbs. Ruminating over the anticipated loss, Tym recalled how the scientists had been perfecting the mushroom varieties for decades but were struggling to maintain adequate yields as new pests and heat stress diminished spore germination. Tym's heart sank as he watched decades of nurturing and careful care become clouded in a thin veil of smoke and heated air.

Tym stood in the stillness of the Gardens alone with his thoughts and the heavy smoke-filled air. It was supposed to be a day like any other: breakfast with his bride, some idle talk about her duties as Queen, working in the shafts until evening, supper usually taken alone because his wife attended to her duties and then bed. They both knew the expectation to produce heirs would fast approach and she was already choosing attendants for her new role as mother, but Tym hoped they would wait just a little bit longer. He wasn't quite prepared to share her with their children just yet. Nor was he ready to give up his work as an engineer to engage in full-time father and husbandly duties in their newly established bower.

Tym moved to the archway that exited the Gardens, sighing at how all their food and hard work would be left behind. An evacuation was eminent. The alarms continued to blare, and judging from the growing heat and smoke, there was no way of stopping the threat. People were crowding every corridor, pushing and shoving against each other in panic. Being so tightly pressed against one another was making it hard to breathe. He could smell the sweat and fear on his neighbours as they moved in one large mass through the tunnels. He tried to suck in some much-needed oxygen and coughed. His lungs were barely expanding due to the tightness of bodies squeezing in around him. Tym kept forcing his way forward. His only thoughts remained on finding his wife.

Before him the large crowd started to thin as his people

dispersed. One of the many exits had been found. As Tym emerged from the smoky heat-drenched turmoil, he saw his Queen, her antennae twitching in the super-heated air. Her segmented body stood unmoving on a flat pebble, with her attendants around her. She was a beacon of hope amongst the disorder and represented the future of their colony's survival. Tym breathed a sigh of relief upon seeing her. He moved to Reyes's side, knowing her by her alluring perfume and said nothing as the massive, towering wall of smoke and fire approached, burning the trees and ground cover in its path. Her expression was unreadable, but he knew her thoughts. Reyes had always had her own theories regarding the changes their colony experienced, but few listened to her. Sharing her notions, Tym agreed that this was connected to the presence of the invasive and monstrous bipeds, with their large machines and noxious fumes wreaking an ever-increasing destruction of the planet, impacting even the tiniest of creatures. As a result, the environment was changing, heating up. The rainy seasons were less frequent and the summers drier, offering less food to forage. The land was becoming more inhospitable and there was little Reyes and the colony could do but flee and adapt.

Her large, tired eyes softened as she turned to him.

"Gather the colony, my love. We must endure yet again," she spoke with a heavy sigh.

Indeed we will, he thought to himself. Tym, as one of the smallest creatures on planet Earth, a *Syntermes dirus* termite living on the edge of the Brazilian rainforest, would endure, as his species always had through the millennia.

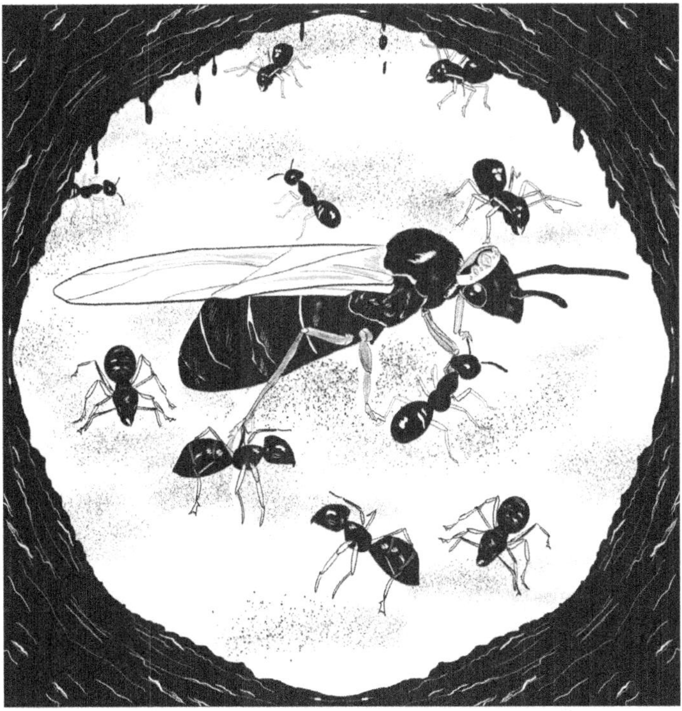

THE GARDEN

BY DAVID PERRYMAN

Georgia (Gigi) Mater's husband died back in 2028 when she was 68. She still has her garden to tend for though. She enjoys growing fruit and vegetables for her children and grandchildren to enjoy. It's reason to see them, and she fears that she may lose contact with them if she doesn't continue with it. It's true, she is seeing less and less of them. The last time she saw her grandchildren was three months ago. She wonders if there is a place for her in their increasingly busy worlds.

One morning, while thinning out the carrots, she starts to hear voices. Nothing specific, just babble. The odd recognisable word, and a *feel* of meaning. But the meaning is unattainable. She phones the doctor.

After many referrals the consensus amongst the doctors is that she is suffering from schizophrenia. The voices aren't threatening, and because they present as babble, there are no immediate concerns. 'Treat it as posh tinnitus,' jokes one consultant dismissively. However, one particular psychologist takes a special interest, and would like to study Gigi more.

Gigi refuses the diagnosis of schizophrenia and insists that it must be an odd form of dementia. It's just voices: they're not telling her to do anything or change her view of reality. It just can't be schizophrenia. 'Dementia. That's what it is,' she tells herself.

Dementia is something more understandable to hold on to and, in a way, she welcomes it: to mitigate the pain she feels from having her family slip from her, she can slip from them instead. But even though the frequency of the *episodes* is increasing, she retains all other faculties. If anything, her mind is sharper than ever before. She develops an uncanny ability to know about current affairs before they're reported. None of the psychometric tests the psychologist presents her with suggest dementia.

Some months pass. They seem like days to Gigi: she measures time from the growing of her vegetables. The psychologist observes that Gigi's schizophrenic episodes seem to pre-empt major events in the world. Messages and babble with the feeling of pain and anger pre-empt a war. Feelings of pride and excitement pre-empt the news of an upcoming mission to Mars. She thinks that Gigi is somehow tapping into world events, and it is manifesting itself in the hearing of voices.

The psychologist persuades Gigi to undergo a series of more formalised tests. Their relationship has blossomed over the months and Gigi is enjoying the attention. In a way she considers the psychologist as a daughter, so is happy to help her.

The tests confirm that Gigi is indeed accurately perceiving world events as they happen. But more than that, she is left with a feeling that there is a darkness looming. Perhaps it is everyone's increasingly busy lives. She doesn't know, just that it's a darkness, a kind of schism, a blankness. It feels very bad.

More surprisingly, the psychologist reveals that the test data is indicating that Gigi appears to be able to steer events! Gigi is not sure how she does this, she has no conscious control, but she cautiously accepts that she can. The evidence from the psychologist's experiments is very compelling.

The psychologist presents a plan whereby Gigi uses her unique power to steer the world from danger, to slow down the busyness. Gigi agrees to try. Maybe, if she can bring the world together her family will come together too. Besides, the psychologist would be really happy if she tried - so why not, if only to make her happy.

The plan is to force an episode by overloading Gigi's senses with news from around the world via every conceivable news source, including social media. In a comfortable room, sitting on a comfortable chair, surrounded by a hundred screens running news from around the world, Gigi lets her mind drift, letting the information pass over her, pass through her and pass into her until she passes out.

*

Gigi is in a space. It is black, a total absence of light and yet she can see. She can sense. She panics and tries to wake up, but she isn't asleep. She tries to move, to pinch herself, but there is no body to move. She realises that she doesn't know why she is here, where here is, or where she was before here. It's as if she has always occupied this space. She has a sense of being, but when she tries to focus on herself the sense dissolves, and yet remains intact. Perhaps she is a ghost?

There are sounds, thoughts maybe; they are what can only be described as 'swirling' around her, through her. She thinks they are her thoughts but at the same time…

Pain… a lot of pain, excruciatingly sharp and then gone as soon as it came. She laughs, uncontrollably. There is no sound. The thoughts form a wall closing in on her, suffocating: she shouts, yells, fights, screams. Laughter again. She passes out.

When she awakes, she feels surrounded by others, and yet she feels the absolute emptiness of total loneliness. The others slipping away when she tries to reach out. A single thought coalesces: 'Gather'.

The thought gives her clarity and purpose: her task is to gather these swirling, elusive, disparate thoughts. One by one she manages to get a hold on the thoughts. She has no concept of the time it takes. Eventually none are left swirling, she has them contained. Again, a single thought emerges from the gathered thoughts: 'Join'.

She must somehow join these gathered thoughts together. Bring them into a whole. By focusing her entire will, she manages to bind the thoughts together into a unified whole. Slotting them into and within each other. The joined thoughts scream that she must: 'Emerge'.

She must emerge from the darkness and find the light. She feels that to emerge she must go up, but there is no 'up' and the thoughts drag her 'down'. In any direction she goes she feels dragged back, or… perhaps she just hasn't moved anywhere. Eventually, she finds a way to think between the gaps of the thoughts and emerges. She emerges into a white space. She feels a sense of embodiment, but still not yet whole.

'Hello.'

A sound, crashing against her, rendering the thoughts into stark throbbing relief. Gigi cries out in pain as the thoughts crash against her. She collapses to a knee.

'It's ok. It'll normalise', Gigi feels a hand on her shoulder. The gentlest of touches. A touch that conveys love and empathy, but a sharpness of pain and regret behind it. Time passes and although the thoughts do not ease, they become manageable to bear.

'I am Balaena. You are being born. You have emerged, but you have not yet become one.'

Belaena explains that she has been here for millennia, she cannot remember when she became 'one'. There are others that have attained oneness, and she has seen others fail or come and then vanish. She has even seen Gigi's species attempt to pass into oneness before, but none have succeeded. She explains that she will use Gigi's reference frames to help Gigi understand what is happening.

'Gigi, I am Whale. I am not *A* Whale, I am Whale. You are becoming Human. You are not *A* Human, you are Human. You see, when you were a singleton, your consciousness arose from the interactions and networks of your neurons. Each neuron took in many inputs and when those excitations reached a certain threshold they would fire, and that output would become one of the many inputs for another neuron. With 85 billion neurons in a human brain those networks of firings gave rise to your singleton consciousness.

'There are 8.5 billion humans on planet Earth. Each human takes in complex information and when that information reaches a certain threshold, they act on it in some way, influencing others. They are like neurons creating networks. The entire human race is a single brain and you, Gigi, are becoming that consciousness.

'There has been a flickering of consciousness' in the past, but your modern technologies have acted like the myelin sheath on the tail of a neuron: In the singleton, it speeds up the communication between neurons, and a consciousness emerges. But for the human race, this speeding up is resulting in many, many competing semi-consciousnesses, barely aware. Clashing against each other, fighting to fulfill their immediate need. Devouring resources to feed that need at an ever-increasing rate. You are destined for madness and destruction. Not just destruction of yourselves, but of all life, across the entire planet. Of me.

'You must become truly one, you must become the disparate thoughts screaming at you. You must bring harmony. You are not being asked to shepherd them, you must *be* them: a single Human consciousness, self-aware and at one. They fight you Gigi. They can destroy you. Destroy your sense of self. But to become them you must totally lose your singularity and become Human.'

'But what happens to *me*?', Gigi asks, 'I am one with the thoughts already, am I not? I am in this place and talking with you so I must already have achieved what is required. I emerged and I have the thoughts under control. I feel them finding peace, what further needs to be done?'

'You are some small part of them, yes. Your journey here subsumed some of them, and your awareness here is as a result – but not all. You still shepherd the majority. To succeed…'

'Yes, you have succeeded!' interjects another voice. 'You can return to your singleton existence now. It's easy. Just blow the thoughts away. Let go. The thoughts will dissipate, and you will fall back. Back to your garden, to your family. You don't want this, trust me. I am Ant, I know about oneness on every level. It is excruciatingly lonely.'

But no. If she does that the World will be enveloped in the darkness she perceived. She must complete her ascension. She must become one with the thoughts, it is not enough to control them. Controlling them is not becoming them. She must become at one with them, even if it will surely destroy any essence of her singleton existence. She decides to embrace the loss of herself. She will die to save everyone.

She chooses to go forward, to be one with all and in the

process risk that she will be destroyed. She knows what to do, she must relax and accept the loneliness of existence. The thoughts stop fighting her, they swirl around her in ever tightening circles, faster and faster, until the white light of their speed explodes in a blinding flash. Except, instead of annihilating Gigi, she remains in the centre. At peace. At one. Human.

Human, and yet, she remains Gigi. A new singularity, but still the old. She has survived and been reborn. The thoughts are gone, subsumed by her. She knows that anything that she thinks will be manifest in the World. If she feels a 'peace', wars will stop. If she relaxes, the World will breathe.

Balaena congratulates her, and others emerge, coalescing from the white to congratulate her.

Gigi has become the human race, a single lonely entity, unifying all. She has ultimate power: she knows that if she reaches to the moon, her touch will spawn a colony. A caress in South America will re-establish the rainforests. A thought to open a window and the air will be cleaned. 'Cool' and the world's temperature will stabilise and reduce. She is all powerful. If she wishes Balaena happiness the oceans will be cleaned.

But although Gigi knows who she has become she has no way of seeing her effect on the world. She is on another plane. She is Human, not *a* human. She has no experience of understanding a single human being any more than a human being has the experience of understanding one of their neurons. She cannot go back to her single human existence now that she is Human. How can she possibly inhabit both planes? And why should she? Ant forms in front of her.

'But Gigi still sits in the psychologist's office. Take what you've learnt back there.'

At first, Gigi refuses. But Ant is correct, Gigi is still there in the psychologist's office. And the crushing realisation that she will never see her children again is overwhelming. She may be able to fix *the* world, but she hasn't fixed *her* world. She can't go back, it's impossible. This makes her feel a sadness that becomes manifest in the world; a deep depression takes over the world's economies. People's lives increase their pace again and they're unable to think about anything other than the 'now'. She has what she needs to save the World, but if her personal world is not whole then the darkness she perceived will prevail.

Ant and many other animal consciousnesses appear before her. They swirl together to form a new consciousness: Animal. Gigi feels a pull to join but is rejected and that pull snaps quickly.

'YOU WILL LEAVE!' it screams. 'YOU WILL LEAVE NOW!'

Gigi feels a physical hand on her corporeal shoulder. Gigi is drawn somewhere, she perceives it as down, but it isn't really a down, it is more of a within and a without at the same time. She senses a true change in her nature, she feels real - or substantial. She has eyes and opens them. Like a sun imploding she inhabits her body. And there she is sitting in the psychologist's lab.

It is the psychologist's hand on her shoulder, 'Perhaps if you close your eyes, you'll find it easier.' No time had passed.

*

Gigi takes the number 37 bus home. On the bus she imagines her children visiting. When she gets home, they are waiting for her! Her daughter explains that her boss had closed the office early and given everyone the day off as a reward for completing a project. Coincidentally, the school had allowed the children home at lunchtime so that a new heating system could be fitted. Her son had a similar story. They'd both seen a meme about mothers and decided to visit, they explain that they hadn't planned it and only found out they were both visiting when they arrived at the same time. The impromptu party went on long into the evening, both her children said they felt calmer and less busy.

*

Gigi has become the master of both worlds, human and Human, whole. She thinks about the things she did in the space with Whale: 'Cool', 'Clean' and they come true. She is no longer lonely. And in becoming whole, she can see light in the future where once there was darkness: a healing where once there was a schism.

Gigi Mater, Earth Mother, continues to tend her gardens.

WASTE

BY MICHAEL CONROY

You peer down at the blood and the feathers. The wire mesh door has been chewed through and bent inwards. Pawprints and bird feet have been scrambling about in the dirt. You pick the dead chickens up by the legs, feathers spattered crimson, and drop them into a sack. Your lower back burns when you bend down. The coyote was infected. There's foam around the mouth. You haul its corpse onto your shoulder, your knees cracking as you brace under its weight. Beside you, the dog scratches his black furry ear. Good boy, you say, and he whines restlessly. You don't know why.

He knows you'd never eat him.

The house stands on a hillside, overlooking the cow's pasture. Behind it, the sun idles in the murky sky, bathing the landscape in sepia light. Down in the valley, a brook babbles softly to itself as one does in old age. The breeze whispers through the long yellow grass.

The cow grazes on tufts of straw in the barren field, only raising its head when the dog darts through the mesh fence.

They're friends, you imagine, the two animals. The cow groans fraily as the dog runs circles around her. Friends, yes, but begrudgingly.

Breathless, you hang the coyote from a meat hook on the outer wall of the woodshed and pace yourself heading back to the house. Warped clapboards hang from the windows and the entire structure seems to tilt to one side, like those queer piles of rocks you find out in the desert – on the brink of tumbling, but still resisting the urge to collapse.

You give a loud whistle and wait for the dog to join you. You sniff your armpit. Foul. The dog agrees – you don't smell your best. You should bathe again soon, though you loathe a cold bath, and the old well hasn't enough water to spare. It's always a risk venturing down into the valley to bathe in the river. There are eyes watching.

The old sweat smell doesn't bother you so much anymore, but your wife deserves better. If you knew how, you'd make her a perfume: the sweetest, richest, longest-lasting perfume a man could make for his wife, of lavender and marigolds and desert lilies, or so you imagine. Truly, there are few sweet smells left to be found. All you know is the hard earth, the electric storms that rise in the east, and to stay out of trouble... trouble being anything that walks on two legs.

Your son saunters up to the fence and swings his legs over. 'Damn things got away,' he says, and runs a hand over his shorn scalp. 'Aren't you angry?'

You squint at the hole in the fence where they chewed through, the lines of blood circling the henhouse. No. There are worse things than coyotes.

The paint on the kitchen walls peels like dead skin around the oil lamps. Dust glints in the light over the wood stove. The curtains above the sink shift quietly in the breeze. Your wife sits at the table, hands in her lap – her check dress is frayed and patched. You sit down opposite, your son between you – he places the rifle before him on the table.

'Is it bad?' she asks and runs her fingers through her dry brown hair. Her eyes catch the light and seem to flicker – like a sparrow's eyes – small and dark, but they glisten. It was her eyes that did it. She's not herself anymore, quieter now – not bright and carefree like before. Every smile a sunrise, every glare an eclipse. You often find her staring at the wall, or out the window, at nothing at all. Not like she used to be. You've been at this for decades now. But one look from her – like a mountain lioness – still stops you in your tracks.

The chickens are all dead, but there should be enough canned food to last through the season. If not, you'll go find some more. You can trade the beaks and feet to the medicine man who comes through this way, plus the coyote pelt should fetch something at market.

She frowns and shakes her head. 'The roads are dangerous, and your leg isn't getting any better.'

Your son places his hands on the table. 'I'll go with him.'

The journey's too long. Someone needs to stay here. Think of your mother.

She sticks you with her eyes. Her voice wavers as it always does when she's worried. 'I can take care of myself, dear. Besides, I'll have the dog to protect me.'

You look at her and then at the dog. He sits in the corner and bites his tail. It's still too dangerous for the boy. You should go alone.

Your son scoffs. His eyes shine like his mother's. 'You can't go alone. We need food.'

You have food.

'It won't last forever. Nothing grows here: the soil's dead, you know that. And what if something happens to you?'

You'll be fine, you tell her.

'And what if you're not?'

A long silence. You turn out your palms.

So, what's the plan?

'We can trade the cow,' your son suggests.

You need the cow for milk.

'We could get at least three goats.'

And who's to say there'll be any goats? Who's to say they won't rob you and kill you and take the cow? Stupid boy.

The boy falls silent. Your wife narrows her eyes at you.

You've survived this long, so why take the chance?

You hang your head, gazing down at the old wooden kitchen table, dull and covered with scratches. You float down into one of the scratches and latch onto a thought. You're running through the grass behind your father's house. He's chasing you… before you got old. You have only vague memories of the before: unnatural tempests, flashes of light and sirens, a world of green and blue on fire, everything falling apart, swept away. Your wife and son stare at you without speaking.

You'll head out tomorrow. You smooth your hand over the stubble of your cheek. The boy will come with you. He holds the rifle barrel like he's paddling a canoe. Put that damn thing away, you tell him.

You kiss your wife on the cheek – she smells like sage. The boy rolls his eyes, hooks his arm through the rifle strap, and heads down to the basement.

*

You prop open the shed door with a block of wood, unfasten your gun belt and drape it over the block. Then you unhook the coyote and lay it down on the dusty ground. It's rare to have found such a specimen. The infection taints the meat – it isn't safe even for dogfood – but the grey-beige fur will make a fine pelt. You run your hands over its side, feeling the skin shift over the ribcage, towards a single bullet wound. It went down easily, all over in a moment.

Inside, you light a kerosene lamp on the workbench. The tiny fire burns your fingertips, so you drop the match and rub it out with your boot heel. It's been some time since you've skinned anything, and the tools seem unfamiliar. You set your knives out in a row ready for sharpening. Unsheathing a small pocket-sized knife, you press your finger against its blunt blade. Pouring a little water onto your whetstone, you drag each knife back and forth over the stone until sharp enough to draw blood.

Behind you, the dog sniffs and pokes his head into the chicken sack by the door. You whistle and he retreats. He's always sticking his nose where he shouldn't.

You tie a leather apron around your waist and pull on a pair of gloves. The leather grips your fingers as in a firm handshake. You can't quite stretch them out – better than cutting one off. Skin yourself, why don't you? Your old skin wouldn't keep anyone warm.

Spreading the fur with one hand, you slide the blade under the skin and cut upwards toward the flank. It cuts smoothly – you're careful not to slice the tendon – the skin offering little resistance. Leg between your knees, you cut towards yourself from the top of the anus and separate the skin from the meat. Blade above the genitalia, you cut along the inside of the leg. Then you grip the edge of the pelt and pull it down all the way. It peels away from the limb, unwrapping its pink-white flesh. You do the same for all four legs, cutting from the elbow away from each paw, cutting upwards, once, twice, and then peeling back the fur.

You tie its legs together and hang the coyote back on its

hook. Trimming the fat around the base of the tail, you take your time pulling down, gradually separating the tail fur. You squeeze a clamp at the base and, gripping the centre of the fur's length, yank it upwards until the tail, pink and naked as a mole rat, slips right out of its covering. After splitting the tail fur, you cut around the belly, then pull down again on all sides until the hide is almost completely inside out. Fatty tissue still clings to the underside of the skin, so you trim the excess and pull down again towards the head.

Blood rolls over your gloves and splashes onto the floor. Your back aches. The breeze cools the sweat as it trickles into your eyes. You blink it away and wipe your forehead with your wrist. The dog whines and watches you, doing his best to look innocent. This'll be you one day, you tell him, gesturing with the knife. The dog barks – don't joke about such things, old man. He doesn't appreciate your wicked sense of humour.

Finding the shallow spot between the coyote's groin and each flank, you pierce the hide with a screwdriver and pull down until the hide meets each elbow. The skin resists at first, not wanting to separate, but relents under pressure. The sound as it peels away – sticky, almost crackling – is like walking through wet leaves.

You cut each leg above the joint and pull down on the hide, exposing the fur underneath, and pull each leg through. You cut around the neck and slice both ears and both eyes, pulling down over the snout and, finally, cut off the nose from the inside out.

When your father showed you how to do this as a boy, you'd nicked the jugular and stained his shirt. He'd broken your wrist for that.

The dog turns tail and flees. You grin and laugh. The coyote hangs before you, its naked body shifting in the wind. The hide in your hands seems alien to the flesh now, as though the animal had been wearing a winter coat. It's no longer a living creature struggling to survive, nor even a thing to be consumed. You sniff the air: nothing but bad meat.

You smooth the pelt in your hands and hang it up to dry. Then you cover the carcass with a tarp and tie it up. You'll dump it somewhere in the woods, somewhere it won't attract any hungry visitors. You used to tell the boy stories about the wild lands, all the highways full of broken cars, and the eyes watching you in the ghost towns.

In the basement, five dusty trays of soil sit on the table beneath a broken heat lamp. You light up two more oil lanterns, illuminating shelves of canned food: pickled vegetables, fruit in syrup, rice and beans, canned meat, canned cake and pudding.

By the stairs, several rusty fuel canisters gather dust. The decrepit old generator sits motionless against the wall. Your shoulder aches. You bend down to a bucket of water and splash your face. It trickles down your neck and soaks your collar and the back of your shirt.

You straighten your back as you dry your face on a towel – and then squint at the shelf of food. After making your selection, you carry dinner back upstairs in the crook of your arm. Your wife thanks you for the food and nods towards the window. You go to see.

Outside, the dog wags his tail with his head in the chicken sack. Damn animal. Should never have rescued him when he was a puppy. You grab an old newspaper from decades ago. *Fuel crisis... Water shortages... Two minutes until midnight.* The grey print and pictures are faded, but it rolls up good and tight. Then you beat the dog's backside with it. He yelps, backing up, head still stuck in the sack. He shakes it off and runs around in circles, leaving a trail of bloody feathers over the ground.

The dog hangs his head in half-feral guilt as you approach, though you know he doesn't understand. He's just hungry. You rub his head and pat his back. He sniffs and licks your hand – wriggles past you, but then he stops. Back straight, ears up, he listens – sniffs the air.

What is it, boy?

The dog stares at you with brown eyes. Then he growls, bites his tail, and chases himself. You scan the fields and trees. It hurts behind your eyes. Too much time spent looking at the clouds; that'll do it. Even now, you can't help yourself but to tilt your head back and gaze at the grey-brown expanse overhead. From behind the clouds, a glint of light catches your eye. It's gone so quickly you're uncertain you saw it at all. And then, like a crack of lightning, a shot rings out.

THE FAIRBOURNE WITCHES

BY MATT BEESON

Look you well to the sea and sky, lest one should fall, and the other rise.

There is yet dust.

Dust and sand, and sea, and sky.

We are out of time. That is, we, my sisters and I, exist outside of time. The breadth of time and space spreads before us, a structure of crystal trunks and boughs that branches into filigree limbs of delicate life: your and our fractal hopes and loves. We are not ordinarily aware of the passage of time, save via its products and effects, those pieces of the crystalline whole that we resolve to set one aside the other, to marvel at the differences and the similarities. The coastline, the mountains, the faces.

On a day such as this, the white horses have riders:

diaphanous ghosts of vapour leant tenuous wisps of life that beat about untethered above the waves. My sisters dance while I wait on the dunes, alone as, sometimes it feels, I always was. Sometimes I look to the sea, but most I look to the land: to the mountains, the sand, and the sweep of the bay, the Friog highland and the Fairbourne low. I look to the people whose lives continue on licence, so long as the sea allows.

There is a boy who braves the weather, seemingly impervious to it, a boy with hair the colour of the dunes on which I stand, the sand beneath my feet. He has curls like wave crests. There is joy here plain to see, spiting the wind and spitting rain, a joy of lightness and innocence as the boy and his father race and chase about these dunes that then and now, I stand upon and look out from. These hills of sand and dunegrass are my humble domain, when I choose to submerge myself and become part of the changing, to feel the whip and tingle of lightness and life, to have it happen to me as it happens to folk. You can see me then if I catch the light on the crest, diffraction patterns just right. But to see me is one thing; to believe in me is another. To know me is something else entirely.

Joining the current can feel like pulling gently on a gossamer thread until it becomes a shroud that I may pull over myself and be drawn into the flow. Nights when the moon is full punctuate the crystalline surface as silver slivers, whiskers in the ice. It is easier to discern these threads and so it is often these that I choose when I feel a need to reassert my corporeality, on nights when my sisters are one in mercury, light skittering over languid waves. And yet, occasionally, as today, I take the trouble to choose the wind and the dance.

The boy laughs and gleefully races up these mutinous dune banks, sliding down almost as far as he climbs, not to be deterred by the surface that slips away beneath his endeavour.

I enjoy the scene and my grasp of the present is lazy and weak, while the flow is turbulent and brisk. Streams meet and reality bleeds, a watercolour with too heavy a wash. There is not one boy but three, occupying the same space and a similar face, at different times: the same path, and the same climb, but separated by decades that present then decay. He always reaches the top, eventually. The summit is nary the goal so much as the race.

At first those faces are the same, then separate yet blended, then with distinction emerging. A coalescence of jaw and cheekbone, they blur and flicker at the edges. Eyes change colour, irises flashing blue, green, dark brown. I stretch and unfold the shroud, and they separate and fully resolve. Set one aside the other, and marvel at the differences and similarities. Even then, to me, the distinction between them is as the rain and the sea, this current or that. The horizon mists and obscures where seas end and skies begin.

There is another who joins late, or early: the man, parent, guardian, grandfather, great or otherwise. He completes the circle with one of these boys, the one who lives, will live closest to the edge. They share a name and dreams of sand and sliding. The latecomer sees me, saw me once or twice, I know. He tells the stories of the witches that live in their dunes and the boys grow up believing in witches and stories and magic and hope in the depths of the darkness. They know the caves in the rockface at village end and the ruined hut in the dunes.

We cannot perceive the whole structure; no matter how we stretch and strain, we cannot understand the whole plan. The crystal branches are mostly less a bifurcation and more a change of surface, with a different curvature. A different texture. Others come and climb the dunes – it is a popular pastime for some folk – but here is a structure, a surface that I return to. I don't know why I come back again and again to this surface almost in preference to any other, save perhaps my idle humming of it, the melody. Or the chord, not fully consonant, an interesting 7th or 9th perhaps, maybe the space between tones chosen sparely. And there is that uncertainty beyond the horizon; as we draw closer to the edge, I want to see how this story ends.

But first this is, almost certainly, how it began.

*

We are out of time, but it was not always thus. I had a youth. I was linear. I did love, once. We, my sisters and I, did love and live. We swam against and across the current until it had no further use for us, nor us for it.

We protect the village here, of course. Or *we* did, at least, and that is the least of what we do. The uncertainty does not stretch to the future of this community, lost as it already is, will be to the waves and tides. But this community came later than many people realise. There was a *before*, at least when we dwell on the plain, putting one foot after the other, living one heartbeat to the next. We predate the village; we were here before even Bermo across the bay. Before we were Fairbourne, we were fair born in the marshes, on the dunes, by the sea. And we were bonny fair.

Few of your kind know the significance of this place. You come to raid the dunes and build your moats and battlements on the beach. The sawtooth fortifications along the shingle top many mistake for sea defences. But they are not; they're people defences, should your enemies come from the west; a relic from a grotesque war that I am given to understand was even greater than the great one that preceded it. Battles are, have been, and will be fought here that decide the fate of the full whole world. They are inflection branches, choices of this future or that. These crystalline boughs draw a distinction without always a difference to us, save in nuance. But not so to you folk. To you the difference is night and day. Life and death. Survival and extinction. To us, one death is much the same as another, but nonetheless we have tried to help, to do our bit. I am, and have been, here, arms raised atop the tallest dune with a battle cry that is the heat of the earth from deep below. I lend my strength to sister Sky as she leads her winged legions against the ice giants that crest the coastal mountains. Their footprints carve the ground and shape it before they retreat and leave the Earth to warm. Our nuance is your matter.

We have a house. You see it as a ruin: the remains of four rough rock walls barely breaching the thigh-length dunegrass. It was once a hut that folk would come to. Even whole it appeared a hut, a perfect square large enough for a horse to stand and turn in, but not to trot in any direction. They would come into the hut when invited. They would stay until they had their fill of counsel or magic. They would see a door in the inside wall opposite the entrance, but if ever they troubled to circle round outside and seek its match, they would only become confused before finding themselves back on the road or the train, or the path across the salt marshes.

Even when we were still more or less linear, we had a sense of it, the whole. The horizon. We could see the line across which we could no longer see. My sister Dylan – as then she was known – brought you to us on a stormy night of our own devising, guiding your path through the current and swell to beach your wreck gently upon the point. You staggered across the sand and shingle mounds to the dunes where I gathered you into the house, and through the door in the inside wall. We were always of a mind, even then, to nudge and change, to pull and prod, so that we could see further and protect for longer.

The Last Horizon

That was why we brought you. This great man. This man of endeavour. To win you and to fashion you to be our implement.

For our weeks and your years, you laid with us and learned from us. We showed you the inner light of Earth, Sea, and Sky. When you left, you left us with hope of a change in surface and texture, and a gift: a gift that would see you live a life extended in length and vigour, and for return on our investment you owed a favour. You were to share our light and dreams with others of your kind so that they would find a way to order the discontinuities and disparate threads into something cohesive or, at least, something other than madness, a sanity sufficient to breast the horizon beyond which we cannot see.

Each of us loved you. Our names defined the manner of our love and the flavour of our devotion. Our names defined our natures from when we were babes, or perhaps our natures bequeathed our names: we were too young to know. Dylan was ever stubborn, irresistible, at times tempestuous. Adaryn was light yet powerful, with a gift for remaining unnoticed, even when plainly visible. And I? I endure. I endure and I wait. When you left, each of us ached for you in our own different way. Dylan suffered with a depth and pressure, Adaryn with a lightness that concealed the weight of her longing, and I, Gwyneth, was ever stoic and patient. As the flows of futures coming washed over us, we became more of our names and less of ourselves.

Three times you returned, will return to us, and each time we asked you:

'What have you done to further the wish of we three, Sky, Earth, and Sea?'

The first time you returned with tokens of a new world. But this world was not new to us, and we were unimpressed. The curvature that obscures your reach is not the same as that which hinders our vision. You answered our question in solemn tones: time did not yet permit. That overwhelming wealth and power must first be gathered so that all would be swept before it. We acknowledged the reason as all clearly might, but even then, as the sighing of the breeze in the dunegrass, the doubts whispered to us.

The second time you came back to us reeking of your success. You spoke of the riches from deep within. We heard nothing save the deepest violation, blackness and death, skewered and extracted, fuelling the madness yet further, sweeping all before it for the glory of more, the maw of more, the morass. You argued, eloquently, of those souls and livelihoods that depended on the opportunity you provided, of the tempo, the timing, the beat, all important to the music of change: 'when the time is right.' But now the time is wrong. It is almost too late.

We saw then, my sisters and I, what ill we had committed to flesh, our best hopes our gross undoing. Dylan raged and the sea surged, washing a storm into the polder marsh. Adaryn became a raven, cawing and flapping, dancing from talon to toe. Dylan staggered to the sea and danced waist deep until her dance and the waves became impossible to distinguish, and her spirit became the spray. Adaryn took to the air, her wingspan, blacker than night, extended and stretched until the sky was her and she was the sky. Such was their grief. They left me here, alone in the hut, tormented by what remained of my stoic hope.

The third time you return, you do not know me. You come compelled, not knowing why. Despite our gift, time has taken pieces of you for the air. I hold your hand and remember yet the love, tempered now with pity. Your eyes rise to mine, clouded and milky. The paper-thin skin loose on the bones of your legs is torn and bleeding from the dunegrass. In your eyes there is a question for which I have no answer but, for all the searching, I can see no regret for the suffering you helped to cause. With a final embrace, I caress an end to your life, and lay what remains down to the dust.

*

It is often said that humans are creatures that live in the past, trapped by nostalgia for truth and better times, but I do not agree. A human is a thing of imagining and dreams, of hopes and fantasies. The muck and mist of what has gone before are the chains and weights that you tie to your wings, all of your own accord. They are not who you *are*.

There are those who say that life begins at the point of conception, but what is that point? Does it begin at the biological union of cells, or does it begin with the idea, the wish for a child? To me, it begins at the point where the only alternative to realisation is grief. Humans are creatures that are as able and willing to mourn the end of an idea, the end of potentiality, as they are to mourn the loss of something material, corporeal. A parent may grieve for a child they have never met and can never hold, who has never even existed outside of their longing. I look out at the horizon and feel myself slipping in and out of this same grief.

*

So, on this day, when Sea and Sky dance in the bay, any sense of the linear, all chains to the surface, scattered and lost, I stand once again atop the dunes, drawn to the current. The boy with hair of wind, waves and sand rambles about, now in full focus. His father – who indeed was himself once the boy – follows behind, steering him along paths where the dunegrass is less dense. For the boy the grass is at head height, more immediate, more likely to sting or catch an eye. The father turns and looks to the mountains behind me, reviewing the scars that the giants left millennia ago. For the briefest moment his eyes focus on me and his forehead furrows, before returning to the chase.

I turn back to the village below. It is built on marshland, reclaimed, low-lying and soon to be lost forever. There is little I can do to defend it from my sister; she and I speak less and less. She is more elemental now than ever before, lost in her own waves. I don't cling to hope so much as support it, and enable it, because without it I would simply cease to exist, and I am not ready for that.

Not yet.

I want to know how the story ends.

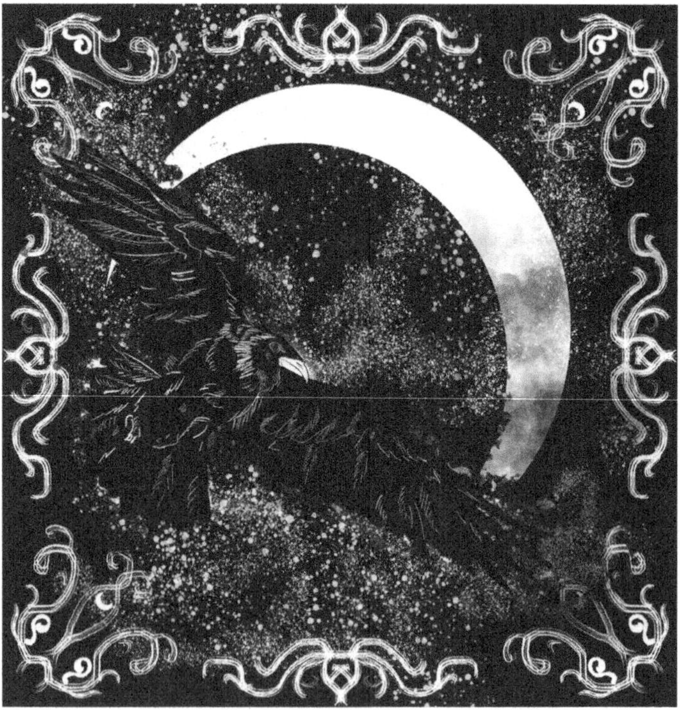

THE SACRED GROVE

BY JOE SMITH

While sobbing at my own warped reflection in the back of a tablespoon last night, my thoughts alighted on a tiresome young woman I once had the misfortune of emotionally manipulating into sharing a cabin with me – much like this one, on this same train, I'm sure. She was a dour-looking waif of a thing, her only redeeming feature being a broad, aquiline nose which appeared to belong somehow to a different face from a different time. She sat there, much like you now, very primly, speaking volubly on a vast and impressive array of subjects – from the Laws of Cricket to the wing venation of a gadfly – but, it seemed to me, nothing she said possessed the merest whit of insight or originality, as if she were simply regurgitating something she'd once read somewhere, in a book perhaps… about cricket and gadflies. That was until, quite out of the blue, she leaned towards me, her eyes bulging like puffball mushrooms, her face white as pure marble, and shared with me something of a more personal nature: a story of such abject horror which, in spite of my cold and impassive temperament, rocked me to my core. It's that story I shall now share with you, *if* you have the time before your next stop... *if*, that is, you're not the sort of person to leave an old woman alone in her cabin with only her spoons, the darkness of her thoughts, and a window out of which to fling herself. You're not? Very good. Then, I'll begin.

It all took place on Anglesey, our story – or Mona, as it was known to the Romans... although, as we'll see, that has no bearing whatsoever on what's to come. Kitty Tuttle, for that was the young lady's name, was visiting the island with her then-fiancé, the equally dreary Charles Featherstone – assistant curator at the Beccles Museum of History and amateur archaeologist – on something of a scavenger hunt after Charles had, he believed, discovered in the writings of a lesser-known Roman annalist named Vivius the exact location of an ancient Druidic grove just a stone's throw inland from the Menai Strait.

Having checked into their hotel on the south of the island, the couple wasted no time at all in setting out for said grove, Charles striding ahead down a winding, yarrow-lined lane to the coast, his map folded beneath his arm and his khaki pantaloons tucked into a pair of thick, woollen socks, while Kitty, struggling to keep up, scurried behind, hitching the hemline of her black ruffle-skirt above her ankles. Did I mention one of her legs was slightly shorter than the other, imperceptibly so? It's unimportant.

Rolling pasture either side of them soon gave way to scrub and dunes, and a gentle breeze, first laced with the sweet vanilla smell of gorse and then earthier tones of damp bracken and cordgrass, stirred the felt brim of Kitty's cloche and cooled her reddening cheeks. The lane narrowed to a sandy path flanked by sea beet and thrift, and when, on the banks of the dunes, Kitty spotted silver-studded blue butterflies flitting between beds of bowing orchids she called out for Charles to look, but he didn't.

Charles ploughed ahead, leading Kitty down a craggy flight of steps to the beach and then along the scalloped shore, where they passed beneath undercut bluffs spider-eyed with dark crevices and topped with heather. Again, Kitty called excitedly to Charles, this time pointing out a pair of snowy-breasted shearwaters perched high upon a narrow rock-shelf and then a company of gannets wheeling in the blue sky above distant shimmering waves, but Charles still didn't stop. Studying his map now, with his forefinger tracing contours and tapping out landmarks, he kept walking, tripping over rock-pools, his feet tangled in wrack.

When the bluffs fell away, he waved impatiently for Kitty to follow and headed back inland, up a trail through the dunes and slacks towards an undulating expanse of shrub and heathland.

Kitty hitched her skirt an inch higher and hurried after him. The ground grew boggy and, more than once, wet mud swallowed her boots to the vamps and seeped through to her stockings. Having to lift her knees waist-high and with her arms pumping, she was sure Charles would've found the sight of her then most unbecoming had he once turned to look, but Charles…

So it was, by the time Kitty reached the solid ground of a short rocky incline bestrewn with bright yellow flowers, she stopped to rest her aching knees and burning haunches as much as to marvel at the vivid flourish embellishing the stone.

Charles, head still buried in his map, vanished over the brow of the incline, only to reappear moments later, peering down at Kitty with pouting lips and fists planted on his hips. His face was unsettlingly owlish: flat and round with a small beaked nose.

'What are you looking at?' he inquired.

Kitty beckoned for him to join her, and Charles bumbled back down the slope, treading on a number of the flowers as he did so.

'Spotted rock-rose,' Kitty told him. 'They're awfully rare. Look, Charles, they're in full bloom – aren't they pretty? They'll flower just once in their lives and then shed their petals a few hours later. We're terribly lucky to see them now... like this.'

Charles nodded. 'You're a fount of knowledge, Kitty. I've always said it – and not always disparagingly.'

'Oh, Charles. Wouldn't it be romantic if we were to stay here a while in the salt air with the waves soughing behind us, watching the petals fall one by one? We might never get such a chance again.'

'Yes, Kitty. Yes, it would. What a lovely thought.' Charles smiled at her and linked his arm in hers. Kitty smiled too. 'Come on,' he snapped, 'we're nearly there now. Just over this ridge'. And, with some considerable force, he yanked Kitty up the stones, their scrambling feet trampling those flowers he'd missed the way down.

Beyond a thick tangle of sedge and flowering heather cresting the rocks, Charles returned his attention to his map briefly before bounding out across the open grassland, counting his every step as he went. After twenty-six groin-straining lunges, he stopped, checked his map once more, and fixed Kitty with a wide-eyed glare.

'This is it,' he spluttered, holding his hand out at his side with his fingers splayed as if he expected the ground to move beneath him any moment. 'The very spot, I'm sure.'

Kitty clapped her hands, raking her eyes over the unremarkable terrain. 'Well *done*, Charles.'

'Here... right here,' Charles began to pace and swing his arms around, 'there would've been a clump of trees. Birches, pale as bones–'

'How idyllic! I can picture it. A slice of paradise.'

'Yes... excrement and gore dripping from the branches, body parts pinned to the bark, the duff sticky with blood.'

'Oh.' Kitty shifted uneasily from foot to foot, instinctively unpicking the treads of her boots from the mud.

'That's what made this place sacred, you see – all the human sacrifices they performed here in the name of some supposed bond with their environment, some sense of transcendental oneness. Oh yes, it filled their fell hearts, Kitty, the way I fill yours, and historical inquiry fills mine. I can picture it too – the birds boiling up from the foliage at the sound of the screams, bloodied hands wielding flints that flashed in the moonlight. Isn't it fascinating?'

'It sounds ghastly.'

'Just a different way of life, Kitty. They didn't understand their place in the world the way we do. Besides, I dare say there's much about our lives that would seem just as ghastly to them. That treacle tart you made for my birthday, for example. A Druid would've probably found that utterly revolting, whereas to me it wasn't. It was fine.'

Kitty pulled her shawl tight around her. 'I don't think I like it here anymore. Is that ragwort over there? Ragwort sap causes *severe* dermatitis, Charles.'

'Somewhere close by,' his eyes narrowed in a way that seemed almost malevolent, 'maybe even where you're standing now, dear, there would've been a stone altar upon which these killings would've taken place. Yes, they would've tied their victims down and–'

'Something like that?' Kitty interrupted, nodding towards a black and wrinkled lump of rock lying like scorched carrion in the long grass thirty yards or so further inland.

'Something like...' Charles squinted in the direction of the outcrop. 'Good heavens!' He glanced at his map, squinted at the outcrop again, and then, stuffing his map into the inside pocket of his jacket, quick-marched towards them. Kitty half-cantered to keep up.

'This is it!' he declared, arriving at the rock and running his hand across its surface as if stroking the withers of some prize stallion. 'The very spot, I'm certain. Here... right here, there would've been a clump of trees. And here's the stone altar, still intact. I've found it! A momentous discovery indeed!'

Kitty, catching her breath, pointed to something white and conical poking from the top of the outcrop. 'What's that there, wedged between the...?'

Almost maniacally, Charles leapt up onto the ledge and pulled at the object with both hands. It came loose. He held it aloft to Kitty. 'Look!'

Kitty squinted, shielding the sun from her eyes with her forearm. 'A conch shell?'

'No, no, it's not.' He jumped back down and showed it to her closely, turning it over in his slight, delicate hands. 'Well, it *is*, but it's much more than that. *Look...*'

Kitty took in the shell's studded spire, the intricate pattern of lines on each of its whorls, the dark orifice of its umbilicus, the glistening pink lips around its aperture. She shrugged and blew out her cheeks. 'It's a conch shell, Charles.'

Charles smiled thinly and shook his head. 'That, my love, is a Druidic offering to the spirit of nature. Vivius writes about something incredibly similar in his annals. Untouched for two millennia – *remarkable*.'

'It doesn't look that old.'

'To the untrained eye, undoubtedly. But I handle ancient artefacts everyday – Norman coins, Tudor spectacles, really old buttons. I'm not supposed to, but I can't resist getting them out of their cabinets. I've received a written warning for it.' He pulled his satchel around so that it hung across his waist and unclipped the flap.

A pang of unease suddenly, and quite irrationally, coursed through Kitty in a shiver. 'It must've been put there for a reason, Charles. Perhaps you should put it back.'

'Nonsense! We don't believe that trifle anymore – bonds and oneness and such. Progress has seen us pluck ourselves from Mother Nature's breast and become distinct, masters of our own destinies. Our understanding of nature has divorced us from it entirely. We are rational, self-aware – there's nothing more unnatural in this world than us, Kitty. *Nothing*.'

'Oh.'

Charles jammed the shell inside his satchel and closed it. 'Besides, I'll be the talk of Beccles after a find like this – the whole of North East Suffolk even. Well, would you look at that… it's starting to rain.' Kitty felt a couple of light drops on her face then and on the nape of her neck. She turned back seaward and saw dark skies that stretched to the offing had crept up on them. A sudden gust of wind pinned her skirt to her legs and knocked the cloche clean from her head.

*

It wasn't until the couple had returned to the hotel that the heavens truly opened, the rain consuming the grounds in a grey, billowy shroud that battered the windows like a swarm of swirling locusts.

At 6pm, the hotel manager announced that the dining room had flooded and, consequently, dinner – roast squab with frisee and pear – would be served to the guests in their rooms. The news was met without objection by all save Charles, who took it very badly indeed. Right there in the foyer, he began to sway, trancelike, from side to side, and, hugging himself, he moaned shrilly, plaintively, like a cat in heat and, much to Kitty's increasing embarrassment, didn't stop until, at last, a well-dressed man with horn-rimmed spectacles and a fearsome moustache stuffed a doily into Charles's mouth and pinched his little nose.

I should've probably told you before – although it's really neither here nor there – that this wasn't the first time since leaving the 'grove' that Charles's behaviour had appeared a spot rummy. He'd had a similar reaction to a number of seemingly innocuous things he and Kitty had encountered on their shortcut back to the hotel: an overgrown laurel bush, a blackbird perched on the arm of a scarecrow, a baize lawn dotted with molehills.

Kitty had, of course, tried to calm him by complaining about the spotted rock-roses and how they'd never get the chance now to watch the petals fall (unless they came back next year, naturally, which she thought they should). But her soothing words had only seemed to amplify his strange, keening outbursts, and when he'd begun to rap his knuckles against his temples like a distressed chimpanzee and foam through his gritted teeth she'd decided to stop trying to help altogether.

Once in his room, though, Kitty again attempted to take Charles's mind off whatever was ailing him by pointing out how irresponsible he'd been to expose them both to so much ragwort, and then by listing all the other harmful plants to which he'd probably exposed them (hensbane, bittersweet…), but, while Charles blinked and nodded and for all intents and purposes appeared to be listening, he soon became distracted by a crane fly which bobbed its way drunkenly across the ceiling and then settled just below the cream-coloured cornice in the far corner.

'…not to mention all those nettles, Charles. I'm surprised we didn't both come out in *hives*!'

'How did that *get* there?' Charles muttered, walking to the corner, peering up at the crane fly.

Kitty sighed. 'I don't know. Through a window? And then there's hogweed, of course–'

Charles wheeled on her, his round face ruddy and twisted. 'All the windows are closed, Kitty! Though they might as well be open. They might as well be. What's the point of a closed window if not to keep the outside from the inside and the inside from the outside? We might as well do away with the glass altogether!'

'We'd be frightfully cold if we did,' Kitty half-chuckled.

'We might as well all blow our noses on the curtains and wipe our feet on doormats.'

'We're supposed to wipe our feet on doormats, Charles.'

Charles frowned. 'I know.'

'Where have you been wiping your feet?'

'Nowhere. On the doormat.' He shook his head, dismissively. 'Yes, we might as well…' And he yanked the small, oak chair out from beneath the dressing table beside him and, approaching the nearest window, raised it above his head.

'Charles, no!'

There was a knock on the door then and Charles froze. A gaunt, po-faced waiter pushing a squeaky-wheeled trolley entered and, with pursed lips and one eyebrow arched, he looked quizzically at Charles for a moment as he squeaked past. Charles, forgetting his rage, pretended suddenly, pathetically, to be inspecting the chair from a number of angles – above his head, out to one side, out to the other – as if he were some sort of hotel furniture connoisseur before, nodding satisfied to himself, he set the chair back on the floor.

The waiter stopped the trolley in the middle of the room and lifted the two silver dome covers from the dinner plates, allowing the warm smell of the squab to fill the room. With a flourish of his wrist, he struck a match and lit two candles, explaining that, unfortunately, the storm had cut the power, so the candles would have to do until an electrician could be summoned in the morning.

'*Bon appetit*,' he smiled, and departed, glancing once, then twice, at the chair upon which Charles was now sitting with his arms limp by his sides and his head lolling back against the rest as if it were the most comfortable chair there ever was.

The door closed.

'Good grief, Charles,' Kitty exclaimed. 'What on earth is wrong with you?'

Charles leapt up from the chair and paced the room. It was getting dark – as dark as our cabin – and the flickering light of the candles danced upon his big, pale face. 'I don't know. I'm not feeling all that tip-top, truth be told.'

'It might be your sinuses. It's a little-known fact that all that mucus production can be *extremely* dehydrating. It can make you delirious.'

'It's not my sinuses, dear.' Charles waved his arms above his head in frustration. 'It's all this… *noise*. I can't hear myself think.'

Kitty looked down at her hands in her lap. 'My breathing is disturbing you again, is it?'

'No, no.'

'Because I've been trying tremendously hard to be less nasal about it.'

'The noise from the… the…' Charles gestured to his old leather satchel on the dressing table with wild, stabbing fingers. There was a desperation in his black, searching eyes the likes of which Kitty had never seen before – except, of course, that time he'd once confused his luncheon knife with his dessert knife at the Country Club gala and everyone had pointed and laughed at him.

'Your bag?' Kitty frowned.

'No. The *thing*. The *thing*.' Charles snatched his satchel and flipped it open.

'The *shell*?'

He removed the conch shell and held it before him as if it were the first time he'd ever seen it. 'Is it?' he asked, distantly. The satchel slipped from his fingers and fell to the floor by his feet.

'I can't hear anything.' Kitty was certain, by now, it must be his sinuses. It was nothing a squirt of saline water in the morning wouldn't solve – you seem sceptical, and without wishing to give too much away, you're right to be.

Vacantly, Charles stared into the shell's aperture then, slowly, deliberately, brought the aperture to his ear, and his eyes spun back in their sockets.

'You mean the noise one hears when holding a shell to the ear? It's just white noise, Charles, background noise our brains usually suppress. A lot of people think it's the echo of the blood rushing around their ears, but it's not. That would be a throb, you see? Charles?'

Charles teetered back and forth, top-heavy on his toes. A long line of drool strung from the corner of his slack, contorted mouth. Kitty rushed to him, prising the shell from his ear. His eyes rolled back into position but seemed now unable to focus. Just when it appeared he might topple over, he steadied himself and groped at the air around him as if struck blind.

'Kitty?'

'What is it, Charles? What's happening?'

'You can hear me?'

'Of course I can. What's wrong?'

'I'm *there*.' He looked all around him then, his glassy eyes touching on intangible things in the darkness of the room, and his pallid, worried face gradually filled with wonder. 'The sacred grove: I'm *there*.'

'You're not. Stop it. You're here with me, in the hotel.'

'I can see it all now – just as I described. Birches, pale as bones. Skinned, severed limbs that twinkle in the moonlight dangling from the boughs. The duff sticky with blood.'

Instinctively, Kitty again lifted her feet from the floor and this time was surprised to find that the rug did indeed feel sticky beneath her slippers – not unlike the floor of this cabin – as if something had been spilled there – syrup or jam... a commuter's breakfast, no doubt. She would have Charles take it up with the manager in the morning.

Charles began shuffling around in the dark, gaping in wonder at things in the room which appeared only to exist in his fevered imagination. Kitty followed him, concerned he might do himself an injury, he might stub his toe on the nest of tables or catch his funny bone on the mantelpiece.

'I can *smell* it too,' he marvelled, drawing in a deep breath through his nose. 'Can't you smell it? The fragrant moistness of the earth, the fresh scent of dewy moss and grass, the saltwind lashing wet bark – all mingled with something foul and putrid, a terrible funk that claws at your throat?'

Kitty sniffed the air, if only to humour him. It was true: the room did smell moist and crisp, but the storm and the age of the building – of this train – could plainly account for that. And, of course, she and Charles had been out all afternoon so it was only natural that certain smells – the wet grass, the sea salt – should still cling to their clothes. There was a funk though, decidedly so. It came to Kitty quite suddenly, hitting her with a gusto that assaulted every inch of her being all at once. Fruitlessly, she pressed her finger to her nose.

'It's the smell of life and death entwined, Kitty, of binaries breaking down and boundaries breached... Of endings and beginnings, and there are no endings or beginnings, no day or night, just the gloaming... An eerie, indefinite gloaming.'

'I think it's the *squab*,' Kitty groaned, edging to the trolley with her finger still to her nose. She put the covers back on the plates but it was too late: the funk was loose and it was set to linger. She made a mental note to add it to her growing litany of complaints for the manager. Yet the smell of that squab had seemed so appetising before…

Charles spread his arms wide and closed his eyes. 'Listen… do you hear that?'

Kitty paused. 'No.'

'A distant owl.'

She listened. 'That's the wheel of the waiter's trolley in the hallway, I'm sure.'

'A hedgehog snuffling in the leaves.'

'That's… now, I've told you I'm trying to be less nasal. You're being cruel.'

'Branches creaking in the breeze.'

'There are no branches, Charles. No breeze. You're here with me in the hotel, and I've had it up to here with–' A sudden gust of wind surged through the room riffling Charles's shirt, sweeping back Kitty's hair, and blowing out the candles. Plunged into an impenetrable darkness, Kitty stood there for a moment, dumbstruck and afraid, until a single thought whelmed her with both relief and frustration in equal measure. There *was* a window open. There had been a window open all along. It explained the wind, the sounds, the smells. It even explained the crane fly for heaven's sake.

With a loud, overly nasal, huff, she stomped past Charles to locate it, but, in the dark, she felt Charles grab her hand and stop her, like this. His fingers were bony and his grip trembled, like mine. When he spoke, his voice was a desperate, rasping whisper. 'They're coming.' He wouldn't let her go – nor I, you.

'Who, Charles? Who's coming?' Kitty's patience was, by now, at an end – sinus-induced delirium or not.

'The *Druids*.'

She scoffed. 'Don't be silly. No one's coming.'

'They're going to sacrifice me. Kitty…' Charles was sobbing. He sniffed and gulped.

'No one is—' Kitty thought she heard a floorboard creak behind her — or a branch perhaps? The sound of our carriage rocking on its rails? She froze.

'Kitty...'

'Shush, Charles.' She listened, cocking her head to the side. The room was still and silent, but she was sure she *felt* something. A presence? The waiter had returned — no, she would've heard his trolley. A ticket collector then, doing the rounds?

'Kitty...' Charles's voice sounded further away now. 'There's something I have to tell you. Before it's too late.' He was over there by the window, near the luggage rack. Her eyes searched for him in the dark. 'When I said your treacle tart was fine, I wasn't being entirely fair. I said it because at that time I'd never tried a treacle tart before and, as such, had nothing with which to compare it. Kitty... please listen to me. I've since tried several treacle tarts from different establishments and yours was not a patch on any of them. I must, therefore, conclude that your treacle tart was, in fact, not fine at all. Kitty, please... your treacle tart was substandard.'

She followed the sound of his voice to the window. No, that wasn't right — she was led there by the cold, bony hand that still gripped hers. In a flash of lightning that fleetingly lit the room, she saw Charles then writhing on the floor by her feet, his wiry arms and legs pinned to the rug by the wisps of shadows. His head thrashed from side to side with a grimace of terror creased across his discoid face. He looked pathetic, wormy and insignificant, and she realised then that she was not only still holding the conch shell but wielding it above her head — the way one might a tablespoon. Her cheeks twitched, her chest swelled, and, fixing you with cold, unfeeling eyes much like mine, she said, if you're not here then you won't feel this...

SEAWEED CITY

BY BOE HUNTRESS

This record, believed to be the work of renegade lifers, was delivered anonymously to our SeaCorp laboratories. Analysis of the record fully discredits its claims.

Seaweed

We spy her from the sea pool. We're singing a mighty canticle – which she rudely ignores, as if we're not chanting ourselves into a frenzy on her behalf. We've been trying to reach her for months. According to the Soracle – who's never been wrong – this young Fleshy, tiptoeing awkwardly across the rocks in her bare feet, is the Onus. So every day we're increasing our efforts – trying to fathom her language. Seaweed, of course, speaks in crackle – imperceptible to the human ear – though most species know every click of the cracklebet (we're renowned as the jokers of the interlace – for a wet breed we can be incredibly dry). But, as everyone knows, languages are less about sound and more about Frequence. It's a matter of *tuning*. And while we can just about locate her Frequence, she cannot seem to meet us there – as though she's suspended between landings. And this, in fact, may be the very heart of the fleshy problem.

We call her Desyr, which is pronounced in crackle as *diz-ear*. It means 'keeper of the well' – a name she's earned for tending to the sea pool every day. Not only does she pick out all the plaz-tek, but she skezches us, intently – like a scholar of seaweed. This of course invokes a flurry of activity every morning: the shaking out of fronds; the over-zealous absorption of seawater (to acquire that swollen pout); the perfect positioning of an alluring recline. Oh yes, we show up in all our glory, in supple purples, and lithesome greens, swirling in the surf like a memorising mural. It's high time we were admired for our intoxicating sensuality. Forget your fleshy sirens! We are the true seducers of the sea. But we are not just glamour and refinement and comeliness – oh no! We are erotic academics – the true professors of the interlace. In fact, there may be no other species as recondite – for we are sages of the liminal, living betwixt the land and the sea. Our brains are a wide open pathway across the sphere. Any fleshy who eats us knows this as a punch packed with nutrients. It's plainly obvious, at least to ourselves, that there's no better candidate for the job – *we* will convert the fleshies. The Onus is ours.

We watch her now, wearing those coral coloured shorts over her brown skinned fronds – of which there are only two, on which she can barely seem to balance. Her hair is a bush of sea moss, ebony in colour, and her eyes are as green and as luminous as any prepossessing algae. It's almost as if the ocean itself runs through those eyes – though she is clearly not a creature of the sea. She has that fleshy smell, like a swell of blubber melting in the sun – and her movements are lumpish, bungling unskilfully through an otherwise symphonic scene.

She sits at the sea pool and takes a skezch-pad out of her

accompanying sack (fleshies are most often encumbered with appendages). As she does so she sings tunelessly. Her melodies move like craggy cliff edges, not rising and falling smoothly like our own – yet we have come to love her songs, just as we have the warped purr of the barnacle, through its sheer familiarity. On any other day we would have merely enjoyed her presence, along with our own, and felt that particular ecstasy of an interspecies melange. But there is no time for hobnobbing today, nor even the luxury of a slow burning romance. The whole of the interlace is buzzing with news of the Onus. Each and every species is trying to decode her oration. The gulls thought they had pieced something together from the symbol on a crizb-pakit, but she didn't notice when we adopted its shape in unison – and the gulls shrieked at us in hilarity, as though we were desperate.

We are desperate. For we have a secret wish that not even the Soracle perceives. We haven't dispersed it on the interlace. This is a seaweed only scoop: we *wish to save the fleshies*. There, we've said it. We itch to preserve them, to shelter them – we crave to become a haven for them, a home in which they'll thrive. For, as we know, without the recovery of the Onus, they will soon be gone.

Our wish is, of course, a controversial notion – not just the enabling of another species in general, but the enabling of the *fleshies* in particular. Their ignorance, their arrogance, their sheer pugnacity makes them abhorrent to many on the interlace – and with no surprise. They have poisoned us all with their pollyshun and their plaz-tek, without a mere nod to those of us who work overtime cleaning the atmosphere. The remaining trees are beyond exasperated, trembling with rage and exhaustion. Long have debates scuffled across the interlace, intensifying as the fleshies ramp up their suicidal efforts. We all want to keep their particular note, their strange shifty singing: yes, even that has a place on the interlace. All species are wanted. And yet, can the fleshies ever learn the meaning of *communion*? Lately, the consensus has been strong – without the recovery of the Onus, they must go – it is them or the rest of us (including them). They've left us with no choice.

But us seaweedians, we believe the fleshies just need a scrupulous kind of influence – *our* influence to be precise. There have been many species, over time, that have created auspicious alliances. Just think of clownfish and anemones, egrets and buffalo, cleaner fish and whales. None of these, of course, were empowering the very assassins of the globo-sphere. But we have looked at this from every angle. Under seaweed skies, the fleshies would no doubt dissolve their brutal rampage and find an inner salubriousness. And no, this is not about us wanting to be *special*, *powerful* or – godosea-forbid – a *saviour*: it's about us feeling a certain kind of calling – one that comes from our fulgent and lustrous nature. We believe we have exactly what it takes to get the fleshies into shape. We are the salt to their sweety, the hook to their catch. We will be the belonging that they crave, and, wrapped within us, they will become beings of a bigger world. To live in the ocean, encased in seaweedian hallways – how could they not fall in love? How could they not move with the rhythms of their own tidal waters and give up, at last, their taste for annihilation?

What we are about to try, as Desyr sits scratching in her book, is a new approach that we've developed through our investigative wit. Over years of study we've gleaned an understanding of the fleshy flaw: *they believe they are separate*. Indeed, unbelievable as it may seem, they have no notion of the interlace – not even as an idea, let alone an experience. It's as if they see the rest of us as a kind of *backdrop*. They do not perceive the exquisite participation, the *intercourse*, the great infatuated love-making that the rest of the sphere is savouring, every moment of every clockless day. And not only that, not only do they separate themselves from the ecstasy of their inter-species eros – but they believe they are separate from *each other* – they believe, each one of them, that they are a *single unit*. And so arises an obsessive compulsion with one another – they are so wrapped up in it – in finding another unit to merge with, or persuading a whole swathe of units of their personal greatness – that they miss the actual and imperishable fact of their own magnitude. It's embarrassing to watch. All of their atrocities come about under the aegis of trying to prove something that is already proven a million times over in the sheer wonder of their existence. They have no sense of their connectedness, and yet they long for it unendingly. And, of course, *we* are all here to guide them, but they have not found their way into the interlace – they are seemingly locked out of it – suspended between doorways, as if their own war of a language disorients them from a clear Frequence.

Our solution is this: we must speak to Desyr as if we are the fleshy she longs for (there is always a special *one* they are looking for). She will never hear us – mere seaweed – because she doesn't care enough about us, no matter how plump or alluring we are. She cannot truly see us, as we are just a pretty and slimy respite from her pain – a consolation as such. But in the *one,* she believes she will find happiness – *arrival* even. Her delusion will not stop until she can consume this thing she believes she has glimpsed but lost. Consumption is her overarching framework, and it never satisfies; in fact it is consuming her – a traitor's lie. Her terror is of emptiness, and yet it is into this that she must go. And we know just how to lead her there.

Slowly, we are taking a form in the sea pool – the form of a fleshy. Not just any fleshy, but the one fleshy that is constantly in her thoughts. We have seen this being, both in living form, and more recently in her Frequence, over and over and over again – like a tide that doesn't move.

At first she doesn't notice – so slow are our movements. But soon she looks at us and she is gasping, her hand slapping across her mouth like a fish kissing. Tears foam in her eyes. She reaches out to touch our fronds, to stroke us lovingly, and we send the joy of it out through the interlace. And suddenly, just as we hoped, Desyr is edging ever closer to the doorway of her Frequence – as she leans into the portal of the sea pool itself – to the emptiness that waits below. She sees the image of her love – the one face that love wears in her eyes (but is writ large across us all). Her Frequence opens, and we spill into it in a flurry – at first, just with the interlace – with *connection,* with the epic sense of oneness between bee and bear and badger and barnacle. And, once we see the recognition on her face – the utter swell of it, then, yes, we add mathematics, we add the alchemical equations that she needs. In short, we show her exactly how to build it. We show her the seaweed city.

*

Desyr

I went to the sea pool every day after I lost my love. I could smell her skin on the salty wind as it caressed my lips, and I would imagine them pressed against hers, cracked as they often were. Her fingers were dry too, like the weathered shells clinging to the rock face. I circled the sea pool singing our song, over and over. I sketched the seaweed because it reminded me of her. She used to pick it at dusk and dry it out in the bathroom so that our place smelt like a fish shop, and then she would crush it up and sprinkle it over every meal, even porridge. She was an ocean creature she said – one with them.

She told me that she came from a seaweed city, and that seaweed had everything within it. "It is flexible, but strong; translucent, but deep," she said, in a sing-song voice. I sucked on her toes while she told me this and thought about how they reminded me of small seals. Sometimes she'd put seaweed in the bath and our skin would grow heavy and soft with it until we became as slippery and firm as kelp ourselves – sliding against one another. She would search attentively on the far-out rocks for jelly bags – the kind of seaweed with bulbous blisters full of goo – and later she would squeeze the gel out of them and slather it all over my hair and my face.

"It's everything!" she would say. "We'll never die. We'll live as seaweed." And I would worship the way her body curved around me, as delicate as the soft hairs covering her body.

I wanted her as an animal hungers, without thought, with a wild kind of instinct. She responded in kind, like she was performing a mating dance, at times moving forwards and then teasingly back, so that we were chasing and catching each other endlessly. She was like the water: I could move within her, and she would open and close around me, sometimes a plunging wave, other times a vast horizon spreading out in all directions.

I adored everything about her. She always sneezed three times in a row, as if her allergies formed a triangle. She ate with her feet on the table, in defiance of her long dead parents – much like the way we lived brazenly on the edge of the sea, despite its constant menace. We watched great chunks of cliff tumble into the waves, whilst shrieking with terror and excitement. The ocean was slowly eating its way to our door. We watched for tidal waves without saying it aloud. We believed we would know somehow, that we'd be warned by our bodies, and flit away with the birds. And yet we watched, knowing that as soon as we could see one with our eyes, it would already be too late. They filled my dreams – watery mammoths pouring into our home, and our lungs – taking us out, our bodies wrapped together as one, to live in her seaweed city.

It wasn't the sea, though, that got her in the end – and she didn't take me with her.

I thought many times about laying down in that sea pool and letting the tide carry me out to her. What else was there to live for now? My life would end soon enough, and what worthwhile thing would I do in the interim? What had killed her would eventually kill me. If not toxus, then the corp would get me. I was a lifer, and they always hunted down their own – for the pennies and the pounds that our bodies were to them. We'd always known they would come for us, and we'd hoped the sea would beat them to it.

When I first met her I worked in the lab and she on the factory floor. We'd glimpsed each other in the canteen and I'd felt the kind of chemistry that, until then, I'd only seen in test-tubes. One night we collided on the roof, both sneaking a rare moment of solitude. We didn't say much, maybe even nothing at all. In my memory we circled each other, like bears, getting closer, rising up on our back legs, and kissing with a tender but urgent fight. A few nights later we concocted the plan: her abandoned childhood home, on a now disappearing island – would they even look for us there? Could we steal enough powdered food for the rest of our short lives? Could I smuggle out my equipment? We knew the penalty for running away. We, like so many, hadn't been able to keep up with the rising price of survival – until the only thing we owned of any value was our capacity to work. I derived great pleasure from my work, but within a prison-like existence, even that had waned – and worse, all the breakthroughs I made belonged to the corp. My knowledge was fuelling their rule. I had helped them discover the seabed as a mineral source, for what I thought would be large-scale renewables. But no, they didn't need to find a solution for the people when they already had us enslaved. They used it for themselves.

The risk was worth it, we decided – we were dead already. All the lifers had contracted toxus – it had started in the factories. We would leave with our souls, and give them to each other for as long as we had left.

Our relationship would forever be imprinted with the adrenaline of our escape. We had anticipated being shot at climbing over the factory wall, but it was the ocean crossing that almost fixed us. Water spilled into our broken boat as we paddled in the dark – swimming and sinking and grabbing at each other. Yet somehow we washed up with all of our supplies, sodden and weeping, onto this chaotic paradise. The feeling of freedom undid us with a delicate agony. Slowly, we settled into the freezing house, to the cries of the curlews, and the never-ending roar of the sea. Every day felt like a heady kind of grace. Building fires, boiling water, making love – life was simple and stark and exquisite.

In the beginning – after the end – I didn't know how to live here without her. I thought about leaving – but where would I go? Here, at the sea pool, she was everywhere, her body a memory dance of picking, smelling, studying. I swear that I began to hear her singing, not with words but with a kind of hum, a low rumbling, like a song of the sea – one made not of water but something equally as substantial. It was a living sound, the peal of grief.

And then one day I saw her – as clear and as true as her own flesh. She was curled up foetally in the sea pool, just as she used to do in the bath, as if she were listening to the still water. I *knew* it was just the seaweed. I knew that. But as I looked and looked I felt the rush of her, as though we were still one, never apart – as though our love was as big as the globe and ran through every species. My heart split open, wider than I even thought possible. And then I saw more: I saw numbers and formulae, and what humans could become. I saw her seaweed city, I saw her walking through it. The walls became mathematical equations – to the point that I began to believe it was possible. I must be going mad, I thought, but I sketched it out nonetheless and showed it to the seaweed – there was no one else to show. I felt their applause like an almighty crackle.

That night I got my equipment out. It had been a long time. In fact, since we'd lived here, I hadn't touched it. It was as if I'd known that I needed to spend every moment with her. And now I was folding out my old life, before her. A life of experiments – of impossible dreams becoming possible. I remembered that delightful feeling of being some kind of magician, the dance between logic and intuition, between thinking and listening – of being a creator.

Ravens sat crooning in my window as I began my research, almost as if they were cheering me on. I became like her – picking at dusk, drying, soaking, until I smelt like a fisherman. Whenever I was with the seaweed I could hear her voice – it became a constant guide. I almost believed her soul was held within the seaweed and we were communicating, like we'd done when making love, wordlessly, full of feeling. Sometimes, at night, I would laugh at what I was attempting – it seemed plainly ridiculous – the hours of time spent trying to forge seaweed into a synthesizable material that would hold form within the sea itself – with vents to let the air in but not the water. It was absurd, I knew it. But in the early mornings I would awaken to a new breakthrough – the liminal space fuelled my madness. My dreams supplied the science.

The seaweed spoke in shapes. I saw pillars in its curves. I learnt to listen to its image-making language, almost like finding a radio station. Once I was tuned in, everything accelerated. I worked in a fever, each piece a clue to the next, and if I listened carefully I swear I could hear the seaweed cackling.

When walking the shoreline, collecting seaweed, I no longer felt alone. It was almost as if the whole beach – not just the creatures, but *everything*, even the sand itself – was speaking. Like we were allies in a spectacle that was much bigger than the world I'd lived in before – one defined by the walls of my own mind. This feeling made me want to find other humans, to share an affinity with them too – I wasn't meant to be an isolated unit. We could live in the seaweed city. We would be safe there, from the corps, and even the tidal waves – as what lives in the ocean cannot be destroyed by it. There would be other runaway lifers; I could fix our broken boat and go find them – risk it, *rescue* people. And we could raise children, free of toxus, free of corps. Everything was here – in the sea, in the earth – not just for survival, but for alliance, for *communion*.

She was my first love, but not my only love. She was the love that opened me, like a portal, to what had always been here – to an interlacing existence. It was the thing that humans had always been trying to create but could never quite let in. What had it taken for me to find it? Only the loss of everything. The deepest love and the deepest grief. The emptiness I'd feared, in the end contained everything I'd ever wanted.

And there came a day, after many days and nights, when I went to the sea pool and I dived in, and I walked through the first door, of the first corridor, of the first seaweed city.

ABOUT THE AUTHORS

MATT BEESON

Matt Beeson (he/him) is father to Brandon, husband to Nola; these are the things that he knows for certain. He is a professional risk consultant, primarily occupied with preventing things from burning down or blowing up. Over the last ten years his focus has been on the clean energy transition. His previous work (not including technical reports and papers) can be found in *The Book of Witches* and *The Book of Demons*, published by Kristell Ink. *The Last Horizon* is his first attempt at supporting the editing and compilation process. In his spare time he likes to read lots of things – his tastes are eclectic – while sitting, preferably. Sometimes just sitting will do. He was once a musician and hopes to be one again someday. Until then there is always chocolate and coffee. He is occasionally to be found on Twitter (@Phaeduck).

J.MCDONALD

J.McDonald is a vegan who enjoys literally hugging trees. Recent publications include "Upon Reflection" from *The Book of Demons* and "A Wake" from *The Book of the Dead*, published by Kristell Ink. Having been fortunate enough to grow up surrounded by the natural beauty of Canada, this author strives to protect the environment through as many small, seemingly inconsequential, ways as possible. For more works by J.McDonald, visit JMcDonaldWorks.com or check out @j.mcdonaldworks on Instagram.

NADINE DALTON-WEST

Nadine Dalton-West is the author of BFS award-shortlisted 'The Women's Song' (in the *Fight Like a Girl* collection), 'Rusalka' (in *The Book of Orm*), 'The House in Brooklyn' (in *The Book of Witches*) and 'Divine Right' (in *The Book of Demons*), all published by Kristell Ink. She is learning to play the cello, and is happiest near animals or large bodies of water. She is on Twitter and Instagram as @andiekarenina.

MARK KIRKBRIDE

Mark Kirkbride lives in Shepperton, UK. He is the author of *The Plot Against Heaven*, *Game Changers of the Apocalypse* and *Satan's Fan Club*. *Game Changers of the Apocalypse* was a semi-finalist in the Kindle Book Awards 2019. His short stories have appeared in *Under the Bed*, *Sci Phi Journal*, *Disclaimer Magazine*, *Flash Fiction Magazine*, *Titanic Terastructures* and *So It Goes: The Literary Journal of the Kurt Vonnegut Memorial Library*. Poetry credits include *Neon*, the *London Reader*, the *Big Issue*, the *Morning Star*, the *Daily Mirror*, *Sein und Werden* and Horror Writers Association chapbooks. He works as a lecturer and as a subtitling editor, which he describes as watching TV under pressure. (Website: markkirkbride.com/ Facebook:https://www.facebook.com/KirkbrideM/ Twitter: https://twitter.com/MarkKirkbride/

JOHN J ERNEST

John J Ernest is an aspiring fantasy author. He spends his days editing video for daytime tv, and squeezing in the odd hour of writing on his debut novel *A Fire in the Night*. When he's not escaping to other realms, John likes to walk around the green spaces of North London, where he lives. His short "The Devil's Tongue" was published in *The Book of Demons* in 2021 (under the name JES Simpson). Tweet him @Geeksimpson or read some of his shorts on JJERNEST.COM, where he intermittently posts updates on the progress of his writing.

JODIE HAMMOND

Jodie Hammond is just starting out on her writing career, eager to see where this adventure takes her. She is currently contributing to this project, as well as being published with her short 'The Weight of One's Heart' in *The Book of the Dead*. Jodie was born and raised in Camden, London. She still lives in the area with her family, her cat, Mog-Mog, and her tortoise, Hissy. Jodie has always been passionate about writing and reading from an early age. She graduated from Middlesex University with a First in BA English in 2021 and is currently studying MA Novel Writing at the same institution. She aspires to go into the world of publishing once she has finished her studies. If you want to keep up to date with Jodie and her projects, please visit her Instagram: @itsjodieee https://www.instagram.com/itsjodieee/

GABRIELA HOUSTON

Gabriela Houston is a London-based writer. She was born in Poland and raised in a book-loving household on the nourishing diet of mythologies, classics and graphic novels. She had spent much of her early school years holed up in the library, only feeling truly herself in the company of Jack London's trappers and Lucy Maud Montgomery's red-headed orphan, among many others. She came to the UK at 19 to follow her passion for literature and she completed her undergraduate and Masters degrees at Royal Holloway, University of London. After her studies she worked in publishing for a few years. She now lives with her family in Harrow, where she pursues her life-long passion for making stuff up. She's the author of Slavic-folklore inspired novels for adults (*The Second Bell*, out with Angry Robot Books) and children (*The Wind Child*, out with Uclan Publishing). Gabriela's website is https://www.gabrielahouston.com/.

A J DALTON

A J Dalton (the 'A' is for Adam) is a prize-winning author of science fiction and fantasy. He has published thirteen books to date, including *The Book of Orm, The Book of Angels, The Book of Dragons, The Book of Witches, The Book of Demons* and *The Book of the Dead* with Kristell Ink, the *Empire of the Saviours* trilogy with Gollancz, *I am a Small God* with Admanga Publishing, and *The Satanic in Science Fiction and Fantasy* with Luna Press Publishing. His website is www.ajdalton.eu, where there is much to entertain fans of SFF. He is to be found hanging out with his cat Cleopatra in London, init.

MATT RYDER

Matt Ryder is a champion of eccentricity, more so with each passing year. He claims he remembers his time in the womb and compares the experience to living in an MRI scanner for nine months. He insists that he is a published author and that the ten-line poem selected for his school's anthology 'most definitely counts'. Once a globetrotter on a mission to discover the planet's most succulent protein (it's snake), Matt currently lives in London with his wife and two sons. He is occasionally to be found on Twitter @Gringlish76.

HUW JAMES

Huw James is a Brit, living in Ireland for most of his adult life, with his partner and too many cats. When not busy doomscrolling, he would be either gardening, or spending excessive time playing video or board games with other humans.

GABRIEL WISDOM

Gabriel Wisdom is a money manager, pilot, former radio disc-jockey, and a fiction writer, www.GabrielWisdom.com. Gabriel's writing credits include *Wisdom on Value Investing,* published by John Wiley & Sons, and 'Demon Rock' (in *The Book of Demons),* a short speculative thriller that takes place at the world's largest free-standing boulder, which split apart in February 2000. For *The Last Horizon,* his short story 'Ancient Dreams' is a techno-thriller about a dormant virus discovered in the melting Siberian permafrost. Wisdom's eco-adventure novel, *Salton Sea Tales* (2023), is part of a PhD in Creative Writing under the supervision of Dr A J Dalton at Middlesex University, London.

JAMIE BEAR

Jamie lives in the countryside and is a passionate vegan. She loves animals and dedicates a large portion of her time to reading. Eventually she would like to own a ranch and rescue animals from slaughter.

STEPHEN BEESON

Stephen Beeson spent his working life helping Massey Ferguson make tractors, and has since retired to a life of watching sports and completing *The Times* crosswords. At time of writing, he has completed 55 consecutively. He is father to two and grandfather to three, some of whom are involved in writing and editing this book. He and Anne – his partner in all things – play folk music more often than is strictly healthy, and retirement has seen his impressive collection of musical instruments develop significantly. He doesn't do Twitter and his Facebook is largely devoted to plugging the folk club he frequents to perform on the third Wednesday of every month. He has always been a prolific songwriter, growing up to the sounds of the Beatles. He also writes the occasional story.

AMIE ANGÈLE BROCHU

Amie Angèle Brochu has over fifteen years of direct social and residential care experience working with vulnerable populations in mental health, education and the non-profit sector. She is currently a sessional lecturer with the School of Social Work at Dalhousie University in Atlantic Canada. From a young age, stories of wizardry and magic have captivated her. Amie is currently undertaking a PhD at Middlesex University London, UK, exploring the progressive potential of fantasy literature in fostering a liminal space contributing to individual, collective and social transformation. When Amie is not researching, writing or teaching she enjoys beachcombing, live theatre, and exploring historical medieval sites. You can usually find her writing in her favourite Muskoka chair with a glass of bubble tea.

The Last Horizon
DAVID PERRYMAN

David Perryman is a husband, father, educator and creator of games. He teaches people how to understand people, how to make games and how to drive narrowboats. David has many published poems and short stories here and there, and even a guide on how to win at one of his games. His writing style is influenced by hard sci-fi and comedy fantasy. One day he'll write a whole novel, just as soon as people no longer need help with the canal lock outside his house.

MICHAEL CONROY

Michael Conroy is a British writer fleeing debt and scandal, on the continent. His current work in progress is a novel about Italy, China, and SARS. Visit his website www.siriuseditorial.wordpress.com for information on editing and copywriting services.

JOE SMITH

Joe Smith lives in Northamptonshire with his wife and three children. He doesn't have any pets – not because he doesn't like animals, but because pets are not permitted under section 12a of his so-called 'tenancy agreement'. When not writing, he is working towards a PhD in Creative Writing at Middlesex University, or staring wistfully out of the window at the family next door rolling around their lawn with their Golden Retriever and laughing – in his opinion – excessively. Twitter: @JosephTSmith99.

The Last Horizon
BOE HUNTRESS

Boe Huntress is a writer, performer and creative mentor living in London. As the 'Artist in Residence' for five years at Union Chapel, voted London's favourite venue in *Time Out*, Boe created a number of immersive mixed-genre shows. Boe is currently working on her first novel, having completed an MA in Creative Writing at Middlesex University. She's been published in *Dancing with the Birdman* a short story collection by Exeter Writers, and has released a number of albums and EPs as a songwriter, having played live on Whispering Bob Harris's BBC Radio 2 folk show. In her spare time Boe enjoys collecting and cooking with seaweed! Website: www.boehuntress.com.

ACKNOWLEDGEMENTS

No work of creativity is an individual exercise, and *The Last Horizon* is no exception. I'd like to thank...

- Sammy HK Smith of Kristell Ink, who didn't say no!
- Kate Coe, for wrestling with the tricky formatting of this book
- Charlotte Pang, who produced the concept for this great book cover (with some final support from Matt and the *Wombo Dream* app)
- Gabriela Houston for the fantastic internal artwork
- A J Dalton for his consistent and honest advice, marvellous editing, and poignant story
- Nadine Dalton-West, Gabriela Houston, Mark Kirkbride, J.McDonald, Boe Huntress, John J Ernest, Jodie Hammond, Matt Ryder, Michael Conroy, Huw James, Gabriel Wisdom, Jamie Bear, Amie Angèle Brochu, Joe Smith, Stephen Beeson, and David Perryman, who handed over a little piece of their soul and being in exchange for immeasurably less than they deserve
- Dr Andrew Detheridge for soil advice
- Nola Dennis Beeson, my lovely and tolerant wife, who somehow continues to allow me the space to pursue my creative and academic goals
- As per the dedication, to all the children who will grow up with the knowledge that they are the generation that needs to do what they can to mitigate and adapt to, and ultimately live with, the effects of climate change

(these acknowledgements written on 18 July 2022, when temperatures are expected to reach 41°C in parts of the UK)
- Last, but never least, Brandon for inspiration and hope

Thank you.
Matt Beeson

A SELECTION OF OTHER TITLES FROM KRISTELL INK

HOLDING ON BY OUR FINGERTIPS

By Kate Coe & Amanda Rutter (eds)

An anthology of science fiction and speculative stories exploring the many different reactions and experiences of people during the 24 hours leading up to the end of the world. Our base instinct is to survive, but when the end is nigh, do we simply lie down and die? Or do we celebrate our life and achievements?

Love, loss, forgiveness, revenge, or just that final goodbye…

With stories from Gaie Sebold – James Everington – Sarah Higbee – Charlotte Bond – Kim Lakin-Smith – Steve Carr – Leontii Cristea – Charlotte Strong – Tabitha Lord – Theo Graham – Adrian Faulkner – Phil Sloman – C.A. Yates – Ren Warom – Terry Grimwood – Scott Hungerford – Courtney Privett

THE BOOK OF WITCHES
By Adam Dalton (ed)

Have you ever been persecuted, demonized, drowned or burnt at the stake? Witches have, and here are their stories.

This exciting new collection brings together the writing talents of international fantasy author A J Dalton, Adam Lively (prize-winning novelist), Nadine Dalton-West (friend to gods and demons), Garry Coulthard (enemy of mediocrity), Isabella Hunter (champion of the unchampioned), Michael Conroy (scion of the Ninth House) and Matt Beeson (right hand of the Guardian of Azeroth) and Michael Victor Bowman (widely worshipped by those who know about such things).

"Contains secrets, magicks, feisty familiars, warnings and true beauty. A must-read!" -Kate Sultrow

MERMAID
By Kate O'Connor

Harvesting seaweed for World Food Co. is the only life genetically engineered sea drone Coral has ever known. Nothing in her short, monotonous life prepared her for a chance meeting with a boatful of strangers who force her to question everything she is. When the opportunity arises to change her place in the world, Coral finds herself caught between a powerful company and the family she was so desperate to leave. Struggling to unravel the tangle of politics and love, time is running out as she fights to learn the hardest lesson of all – what it means to be truly human.

AUTONOMY

By Jude Houghton

Balmoral Murraine works in a Battery, assembling devices she doesn't understand for starvation pay. Pasco Eborgersen is the pampered son of an Elite, trying to navigate the temptations of the Pleasure Houses, the self-sacrifice of the Faith, and the high-octane excitement of Steel Ball. They are two strangers, who never should have met, and now they will rip apart the world.

What happens when ninety percent of the world lives on skaatch – a jellyfish and insect composite? What happens when mankind spends more time in alternative life sims instead of in the "real" world? What happens when economic interest is the sole determinant of global decision making? What happens when a single secret is discovered that calls into question everything we have ever believed?

Welcome to the Autonomy. Welcome to your future.

THE BOOK OF DEMONS

By Adam Dalton (ed)

What if I offered you the words to conjure a demon? And what if that demon could provide you with everything you'd ever wanted?

Shall I whisper the words now? Come on. What harm can it do?

This new collection brings together the writing talents of prize-winning fantasy author A J Dalton, Nadine Dalton-West (friend to gods and demons), Isabella Hunter (champion of the unchampioned), Michael Conroy (scion of the Ninth House), Matt Beeson (right hand of the Guardian of Mizeroth), Nozomi Okumura (disembodied dramaturge), Gabriel Wisdom (High Lord of the Lower Realm), JES Simpson (eldritch scribbler), Elyn Joy (First Handmaiden of the Protocosmos) and J.McDonald (Canadian).

INFINITE DYSMORPHIA

By Kate Coe & Peter Sutton (eds)

An anthology of science fiction and speculative stories exploring how science and technology could change what it means to be human. Bio implants, cybernetics, genetic modification, age reversal, robotics and technology…what is the human experience of undergoing these procedures, and what is the advance of technology going to bring?

What does the future hold in store for those who are pushing the definition of humanity?

With stories from Ren Warom – David Boop – Isha Crowe – Dolly Garland – Thomas J. Spargo – Elizabeth Hosang – Ron Wingrove – Sean Grigsby – Courtney M. Privett – Steve Cotterill – Anne Nicholls – David Sarsfield – Frances Kay – Alec McQuay

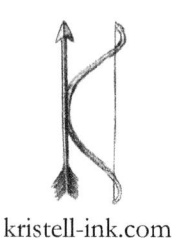

kristell-ink.com

Printed in Great Britain
by Amazon